The Situe Stories

Arab American Writing

The Situe Stories

FRANCES KHIRALLAH NOBLE

 Syracuse University Press

First Edition 2000

00 01 02 03 04 05 06   7 6 5 4 3 2 1

The paper used in this publication meets the minimum requirements of American National
Standard for Information Sciences—Permanence of Paper for Printed Library Materials,
ANSI Z39.48-1984. ♾™

Library of Congress Cataloging-in-Publication Data

Noble, Frances Khirallah.

   The Situe Stories / Frances Khirallah Noble.

      p.   cm.—(Arab American writing)

   Contents: Situe—Albert and Esene—Genevieve—The war—The table—The
American way—The hike to Heart Rock—Sustenance—Dry goods—Kahlil Gibran
—The honor of her presence.

   ISBN 0-8156-0657-5 (alk. paper)

   1. United States—Social life and customs—20th century—Fiction.   2. Arab
Americans—Fiction.   I. Title.   II. Series.

PS3564.O236 S58 2000

813'.6—dc21   00-030779

This book is dedicated to my *situe,*
Elizabeth Feres Abraham

I also offer special thanks to other *situes* I have known:
to Genevieve Abraham Casino,
to Olga Abraham Ellis,
to Amelia Massoud Karma Abraham,
to Gladys Shibley Sadd,
and to Emma Abraham Shibley.

Frances Khirallah Noble is a lawyer and writer. She lives in Southern California with her husband and son and daughter.

Contents

Acknowledgments

First, of course, my loving thanks to my husband, Tom, who supported me in every way in my decision to change careers and become a writer at a somewhat later stage in life. Simply put, none of my work would have been possible without him.

Other thanks are also due: to my son, Ian, and my daughter, Maureen, who were continually encouraging and often first readers of the stories; to Anne Zwicker Kerr for generously recommending the book to Syracuse University Press; to Virginia Tufte, my former English professor and my friend; to Gladys Shibley Sadd for providing a wonderful resource in her book *The Wit and Wisdom of the Middle East* and for the afternoons she spent telling me of the old country; to Genevieve Casino, who shared stories with me; to Denny Luria, Carla Saunders, and Carol Silbergeld for their support and encouragement over the years, with additional thanks to Denny Luria for her assistance in the preparation of the manuscript. Finally, thanks to Mary Selden Evans of Syracuse University Press for her enthusiasm and perseverance in bringing the manuscript to publication.

A Note to the Reader

Situe is the Arabic word for grandmother. Although all eleven stories were inspired by my own and other *situes*, only the first and last stories overlap—pillars for the century of experience described in between. The other nine stories contain different *situe* characters: some called "Situe," some by their given names, some by both. Throughout the collection, I often gave the name "Hasna" to a story's *situe* character because the name Hasna is, for me, particularly resonant and evocative.

The Situe Stories

Situe

Hasna's father died of a stroke and barely a tear was shed. Hasna, a baby, didn't know that she should cry. Her mother had learned not to. Her four older brothers, half a world away, received the news too late to mourn. The neighbors? For them, the luxury of painless concern: they were good people, it was a small village, Hasna's father had passed his prime.

Ah, but Situe, Hasna's grandmother, and the mother of the deceased, propped her wooden chair in the shade of her porch and sat, eyes wet and down, until her son was buried in his grave at the bottom of the hillside olive grove.

Within a week, the fever took Hasna's hair. It raged relentlessly for four days over the balding child; Hasna's mother, driven to despair, hid the black curls in a clean muslin cloth in the bottom of a dresser by the window.

All the while, Situe moved like a dervish between the

stilled mother and ravaged daughter. She sponged the baby and put the mother to bed. She beseeched God to "save Hasna, save Hasna."

Round and round, Situe gently rubbed the baby's head; first with a cold towel to lower the fever, then with her finger dipped in olive oil so the heated scalp wouldn't crack. Situe rubbed and rubbed until the febrile head seemed to vibrate from her touch: that perfectly round head, so naked and smooth.

To measure how much good she was doing, Situe read the baby's fortune in cards. Just ordinary playing cards whose power depended upon the user. But this time she couldn't read what was coming.

She didn't know if she would save her. As her solemn eyes roved over the child, she asked God for a sign and looked forward to sleep, thinking God might give her an answer then.

Once when she'd been very sick herself, her dead husband appeared to her in a dream and told her to come with him, he was so lonely. "No, Ibrahim," she'd said in the dream. "Not yet." From that time on, she knew she would recover.

In the morning, Situe carried coffee to her dry-eyed daughter-in-law, left worn and weak by this third trial so close on the heels of the second. Crying hadn't stopped her sons from riding in the cart to the ocean, from boarding the ship, from traveling out of her future. Crying wouldn't have saved Hasna's father or Hasna's hair: he—and it—were gone before she knew it.

If asked where her sons were, Hasna's mother responded flatly, "In Boston in the United States of America."

When asked why, she gave a faltering answer, often different from the one she'd given before. She said, "Because they thought our village was drying up," or "Because they forgot I would dry up without them." She could have added, "They wanted me to go, but I couldn't. I'd have left too much of myself behind." She'd look around at her questioners and add, "Have you tried to untangle the grapevines? Too much tearing and they die. Pull them apart and they bleed."

When Hasna didn't revive in another day, Situe called in the others. They sat in silence in the warm, dry room. Each had a remedy.

A poultice.

A special tea.

An incantation.

A child came to the door, looking for his grandmother.

"Situe?"

"Eh?"

They all looked up. Six sets of sable eyes in dark, creviced skin darkened further by the vigilant Syrian sun.

One tried to read Hasna's fortune in her coffee grounds, but could only go so far, so she mixed her finger around in the bottom of her cup to conceal her failure.

Another, famous for her predictions on recovery from near-fatal illness, said, "I cannot see what will happen to this child.

She won't awake from the fever?

The old grandmother shrugged.

When Situe returned to her solitary vigil, she again dipped her finger in the candle-warmed oil. And rubbed. This time, on faith alone. She started over the child's right eyebrow and moved to the crown of her head, the side, back and forth—drawing eggs of various sizes, and the moon, the sun, the pebbles at the seashore. When her finger went numb and her wrist refused to direct the motion, she changed hands—for hour after hour as some in the village waited for news of another death from the melancholy house.

But Hasna defied them all.

In the middle of the night, her voice invaded the air.

Out from under the thickness of covers. Struggling against the abundance of pillows. Hasna. Wailing and bellowing.

Situe scurried for food as she called to Hasna's mother to wake up, a miracle! a miracle! Go see the baby! Look at our Hasna!

Hasna, the resurrected. Hasna, the triumphant. The unbound, the strong. The names went on and on and the list grew as she did: the unpunishable, the unaccountable, the defiant, the willful, the adventurer.

Hasna gobbled yogurt and cucumber, a handful of rice, a mouthful of chopped spinach splashed with lemon juice, butter, cinnamon, allspice. She ate kibbe wrapped in Situe's hand-rolled bread. She fought her mother for the mirror and looked at her drawn cheeks and her bald head and laughed without control until, once again, she fell asleep. As Situe herself finally did, her head hanging forward like a lily drooping on a stem.

Hasna remained hairless in a society of thick, dark manes. Six months, a year, and more years, until she approached womanhood with the sleek head of a statue. Situe continued to rub, rub.

Mothers explained to their younger children, "God tried to pull Hasna into heaven by her hair, but Situe said no and pulled her back."

Allowances were made for her. The men let her watch when they played cards and ate *fatteh bi-zeit*. Hasna tasted the garbanzo bean mixture as soon as it was made and teased the men when they lost. In memory of her father, they gave her a coin from each pile of their winnings.

Like the other girls, Hasna worked at home helping her mother. She worked in the vegetable plot among glistening eggplants. She made olive oil at her family's olive press and tended the olive grove with her cousins. She went to church and acted in the holy day plays, although when it came time to hand out the parts, there was the usual difficulty: boy? or girl? head covered or not? She was tall, beautiful, muscular, bald.

But while the other girls adorned each other's hair with combs carved from wood and inlaid with mother of pearl; while they groomed themselves with scented pomades as they listened to their parents planning their engagements—Hasna groomed her horse.

A golden Arabian as a gift from her absent brothers.

A golden Arabian with brown eyes.

"Like mine," Hasna said.

"Don't get carried away," the other girls commented. "All horses have brown eyes."

"Except albinos."

"And they're freaks of nature."

Like a hurricane, Hasna rode her stallion over the hills, across the small valleys, and down the steep narrow streets of her village. She frightened people from the footpaths. The men said it was because she didn't a have a father to contain her. The women pointed to her passive, pliant mother.

Situe said nothing, but for Hasna's thirteenth birthday, she braided a golden bridle to match her golden horse.

And all the while, Situe rubbed. In the evenings after dinner, Hasna laid her head in Situe's lap, while her grandmother summoned magic. Hair appeared in other places, but not on her head. Still, Situe rubbed. Her hands, for an old woman's, were handsome and her nails smooth as ivory. Her black diamond ring caught the light from the oil lamp in the corner.

Some time thereafter—no one remembering for sure except Situe—the beginnings of hair appeared on Hasna's head. Like the down of a baby chick at first. Evenly distributed around her face like a halo. Fine, straight hair. As it grew, it became coarser and thicker. At about four inches, by its own weight, it dropped toward her shoulders, and the slightest wave appeared.

"Baby hair is sometimes lighter when it comes in," said her neighbors. "Before it darkens."

"Hasna's not a baby anymore," was the answer.

For there was no denying it, Hasna's hair was lighter than it used to be. Very light. Light itself. The first such head of hair in her family or in the village in any genera-tion. Gold, goldenrod, lightning rod. Long, coarse. Gold—like the horse's tail that streamed behind her when she and her stallion raced by.

One day a letter arrived from the second of Hasna's older brothers. The village priest read it aloud to them: would Hasna like to come to visit? And here is some money to get what you need.

"I want to see my brothers," Hasna said.

Situe, in her old chair on her porch, smoke escaping from her mouth and the bowl of her white china pipe, ex-tended her hand to Hasna.

"Puff?"

"Just one . . . or two."

It was decided that Hasna would go. Hasna's mother slept for a day and a night before starting to sew the clothes

Hasna would need. More often than not, Situe sat silently in her chair, her granddaughter's golden light extending and deepening as her own began to fade—as she settled for two meals and picked at the third, as she overlooked a little dust inside her doorway.

A week before her departure, Hasna announced that she would use the money her brothers sent her to buy passage for her horse.

"A horse at sea?"

"On a ship crowded with people?"

"She's cracked."

"Like an egg."

On the day Hasna was to depart, the driver of the cart arrived early, so her mother gave him coffee and figs. Afterward, the driver, showing off his muscular back and arms to the woman whose hair was an intriguing mystery to him, lifted Hasna's trunk like it was a matchbox and set it in the back of the cart. He did the same with the bale of hay.

The entire village turned out to say good-bye. The jealous, the curious, Hasna's family and friends. The sincere young man whose advances Hasna rejected with bemusement; the rowdier ones who never adjusted to Hasna's transformation from object of scorn to object of desire. Father Khoury sprinkled holy water on the trunk, the hay, the unwilling driver. He blessed Hasna and her horse and the horse that pulled the cart.

Hasna's mother in her finest clothes presided over the event. On her orders, her nephews and nieces passed out kibbe and bread to the crowd; they set up the coffee urn and opened bottles of wine. At the end, she approached her daughter and inhaled Hasna's scent one last time, unable to give the speech she had planned. Then, stepping back from the spirited horse, she watched Hasna mount, and fly up the trail far ahead of the cart and its stolid driver. She waved as Hasna circled, returned, and rode off again. Hasna—using every equestrian flourish at her command. Until in the dim distance the horse and rider took the form of a traveling spot of dust, approaching, revolving around, and departing in silence from a slower one. Hasna's mother and a few of the others stayed until the spots disappeared.

Situe, on her porch, in her chair—the place she occupied during the festivities—felt every turn and jolt of Hasna's journey. As if she and Hasna were connected by an invisible thread. Every tug reminded her that Hasna had stopped to rest, or was climbing a hill, or watering her horse. Hours later, when Hasna reached the shore, the wisps of Situe's white hair almost lifted with the wings of the seabirds. And when the horse balked for an instant before boarding the ship, Situe's heart smarted and pinched. And when Hasna led the way up the gangplank and crossed the threshold of the vessel, the rest of the invisible thread peacefully unwound, leaving an empty spool.

The Situe who believed in dreams greeted her husband without surprise.

When the neighbors found Situe's empty body, she was weightless as a cocoon. They swore she could have blown away like a feather.

"It's a measure of her soul," said the grandmothers.

"Solid and heavy as gold."

They laid her out and sat in reception in a line of chairs beside her, silently offering Situe's daughter-in-law a wall of comfort as she cried quietly in her shawl.

"A good sign," they agreed.

Meanwhile, Hasna's joy at sea exceeded that of every other passenger. She scooped horse manure and tossed it into the ocean with abandon. She faced west into the wind. At sunset each night, as she inhaled the freeing air, she sent prayers and love to Situe and her mother.

Once, in the instant before the sun disappeared into the ocean, she saw the flash of green that the crew said appeared to a lucky few. Students of nature and believers in God, they argued whether the flash was due to renegade lightning or spirits with no place to go. The mystery, though, to all of them, was, why green? Why not orange or red or yellow, the colors of the sun?

"Reflections from the sea," offered the first mate, who hovered around Hasna and helped her brush her horse.

"A distortion of the blue of the sky," suggested another.

"Or the imagination."

"It is what it is," said Hasna, as she patted the rump of her valiant stallion.

"Our priest could explain it," said the admiring first mate. "He understands God and nature. And magic."

Hasna said, "Situe says they're all the same thing. And if they're not, who can tell? And if nobody can tell, what does it matter?"

Then to the astonishment of those present, Hasna lit her first pipe at sea. The little white china pipe with the perfectly round bowl. She said, "Situe gave this to me before I left. It's mine to use however I want." And she inhaled deeply, letting the smoke float out her half-smiling mouth.

She extended the stem toward the lips of the first mate—a strong, dark man with heavy-lidded hazel eyes. He accepted, drawing the smoke through the porcelain straw as the kernel of burning tobacco in the end of the pipe glowed brighter. After a couple of puffs, he returned the pipe to Hasna's open hand.

In the deepening darkness, the small crowd around them dissolved like the smoke that escaped from their mouths and nostrils before being spirited away in the winds. The evening chilled. The pipe warmed. Hasna and the first mate stayed on deck, the last to leave. When they finished smoking, Hasna tapped the remains of the tobacco over the ship's railing and tucked the pipe in the pocket of her long, loose skirt. She asked the first mate whether he spent much time on land.

While Hasna slept that night, as the ship rolled and groaned, Situe appeared in her dreams: there, on the porch, in the chair, holding the pipe. Still and calm. Breathing in. Breathing out. In. Out. In. Out.

In.

Out.

In.

Out.

Albert and Esene

They sat side by side in the living room of the small duplex, their short, white legs without demarcation for ankle or calf—identical legs, except that one pair was plump and the other, thin—hanging over the side of the couch. Their feet barely grazed the floor. In a rare convergence, they had agreed that the occasion called for their good black dresses. Amelia and Safiyah, in dignity and forbearance, visiting Esene.

The husband of Esene had died two weeks before. His sisters, also widows, had come to console. And to have lunch. Already the smells for which Esene was known floated from her kitchen to reassure her neighbors that she was recovered enough to cook.

Esene carried two mugs of coffee into the living room.

"Did you put cream and sugar?" asked Safiyah.

"I know how you like it," answered Esene.

14

"I don't see how you can drink coffee in this heat," complained Amelia, her vast and magnificent bosom rising like bread dough above her dropped neckline. "Usually it wakes me up, but in this heat, it makes me so tired."

"If anyone should be tired," Safiyah said, "it should be me. I drove us all the way up here."

"You slam on the brakes every time you see a car," Amelia accused, and she inclined toward Esene, pretending to be confidential. "People were honking and shouting at us the whole trip and she didn't notice. Stop. Start. Stop. Start. She stops twenty feet before every intersection." Then she turned to Safiyah. "This is the last time I let you drive me anywhere."

"He who digs a pit is likely to fall into it," Safiyah answered, subsiding into her sweetened coffee. "Who'll drive you if I don't?" And she clutched the cup with her bony hands, her perfect red fingernails, like pyracantha berries blazing against the white glass, her diamond rings weighting her fingers.

"At any rate," Amelia began again, "now we're all the same. Floating in the same boat, eh, Esene? Safiyah and I, we can tell you what it's like to be a widow."

Esene. Who'd taken the armchair by the window, stepping past the pile of unfolded newspapers and untouched magazines that tilted against the leg of the television. Esene. Crocheting. Cream thread growing into a doily. Defeating Amelia's attempts to encircle her with her defeating smile.

For sixty-two years, Esene had paid little attention to her sisters-in-law. This, on the advice of her husband when she'd asked how to approach the women into whose family she had intruded. "Don't get drawn into it," he'd said. "It's the only way they know how to speak. If you say little," Albert wisely counseled in the face of their outstretched arms, the imbroglio of their embraces, the Sunday feasts, the shirts off their backs, "and act less, they'll think you agree with them. No one will argue. There'll be no one to convince. Or, if you prefer," he brushed his luxuriant black mustache with the tip of his finger, "I'll do the talking for both of us."

Which is what he did.

"She's like a silent child," his family said. "Not a thought in her head. It's probably a good thing they have no children." This was Esene's only real sadness. Not that Albert wasn't vigorous and passionate in bed. Not that Esene didn't respond, urging him. Everyone in Albert's family blamed Esene. Her family, distant by the width of a country, ceased to think about faraway grandchildren, until Esene existed for them primarily as the exotic aunt in California who mailed five-dollar bills in Christmas cards written in pencil in her large, coarse script.

For Albert (whom they had met but once) had taught her to read and write.

At first he had merely read to her every night from the evening papers, adjusting the position of his magnifying glass for the Arabic or English letters, railing against the injustices reported from around the world. Esene sat like a cat on the rug next to his chair, her head pressing against his knee.

One night he proclaimed, "Esene, I'm going to teach you to read!"

"Albert," she laughed. "Why?"

"The women in this country read."

With the same fervor that led him to stock his tiny Arabic grocery store with Coca-Cola, American cigarettes and magazines and candy, and to encourage his customers to speak English on the premises (if they could) every other Monday, he set out to teach Esene to read. She was thirty-five years old and much younger than he.

"At . . . bat . . . cat . . . This is so silly."

"Here, Esene, smoke, if it helps you relax . . ."

Shades drawn. Front door locked. To prevent discovery,

because Albert wanted it to be a surprise, his surprise to unveil like a repainted statue. It was not to humiliate his sister, Amelia, who had received their mother's recipes, wordlessly, by watching and doing; who handed over to her husband without a glance all written matter; and who argued day and night with that husband over what her mother said, his sister said, what they should do, where they should go, while she expanded and puffed up until he resentfully wondered how much larger she could grow. Nor to spite Safiyah: wealthy by marriage, with her diamonds and her sheared fox wrap, whose empty head held jet stones in place of eyes and whose teeth clenched its own paws in a ring around Safiyah's elegant neck. It was certainly not to defy Albert's mother, Hasna—no, he was her favorite and he basked in her affectionate glow.

When Esene asked again, "Why, Albert?" he merely laughed and pushed her nose into a book. "Our secret," he reminded her.

Esene pronounced "tin, fin . . . bob, cob . . ." from lists of Albert's devising. Then words from a child's book that Albert searched for in the library, a book that would not cause Esene to bristle with impatience.

"You must be diligent," he instructed. "You must work every day."

"I will not miss my programs," she snapped, leaving the theme book, the pencils adrift on the couch with elaborate indifference. For one day, then two, while she expanded her radio listening to cover every available hour.

"But how will you be ready?" Albert asked. "Christmas is coming and you won't be ready. What about our plan—"

"—Your plan, Albert!"

"—to send out American Christmas cards for the first time. In your hand. Which you will write. You'll surprise them all, Esene . . . Please."

But, for the time being, Esene said, she wanted to revive her afternoon card games with her friends, who'd wondered at her unavailability—that is, if she still had any friends, she said to him morosely; if they hadn't disappeared in the labyrinth of her many absences.

"But, Esene, you only study in the evening. You've had plenty of time for your friends."

"You don't know what I do all day," Esene sobbed. And she gathered herself to parade down the sidewalk, past the small, respectable house of Albert's mother, Safiyah's large two-story house, and Amelia's white frame cottage, nestled in a court of six equivalent structures—without a glance in their direction—to social events to which they were not invited.

"She looks different coming and going," said Safiyah.

"Less steady on her feet," Amelia observed.

"Slower."

"Drunk."

"Albert indulges her."

"Is ruled by her, you mean."

If Albert came home early, he tucked her in bed himself, tasting the lovely bourbon on her lips (which the women around the card table sipped from crystal shot glasses), slipping off her navy dress, unrolling her stockings, sliding his hands over her olive-skinned body, releasing the combs in her hair. He pulled down the shades; he loved her easily and languorously, so that before they'd finished, she was nearly asleep. Afterward, he lay on his back in their mahogany bed and pulled the covers over his face. It was the way he always slept.

As December approached, Albert increased the pace of the lessons: three- and four-syllable words in sentences, the use of the comma, the closing of a letter.

"All you need to know is enough to sign the Christmas cards," he badgered impatiently. "And write a short message." Esene adamantly refused to use a pen; they smeared and could not be erased. Albert shopped for cards they could afford, with space enough to accommodate Esene's expansive script.

As for Esene, even through she didn't love to study, even though Albert pushed and prodded her, she began to realize the power of what she was doing. She could hardly keep quiet. Words she knew floated all around her—in shop windows, on street signs, in magazines, newspapers, on packages, at church. Words she could read sat on the tip of her tongue, ready to leap off at any moment. What could she do? Deny what she knew? What was becoming automatic? Almost beyond her control? Esene's secret knowledge had begun to burn like a hot potato in her stomach; like a fox gnarling.

Albert tried to remind her: "Remember, it's our secret for now."

"Yes, yes, Albert. I know. I know."

Still, Esene stuffed magazines at the top of her shopping bag, allowing the corner fringes to peek over the edges. She asked out loud in front of Safiyah and Amelia, "Where is your Sunday paper?" Adding, after a moment's taunting silence, "For Albert."

On an evening several days before the cards were to be written and mailed, retrieved from the safety of their hid-ing place in the space under the kitchen sink, Esene said to old Nasef, Albert's father, who was deaf and nearly blind, "Would you like me to read you a story?" Then she turned to Albert, whose heart had made an invisible leap, and said, "Did I startle you?"

One morning soon after, the family set out to visit an ailing third cousin who'd arrived from Boston to winter in the paradise that was Los Angeles—warm, uncluttered, like the old country, healing to the joints and lungs, where the familiarity of oranges, grapes, and dates grew along the streets and in the vast spaces between buildings. Everyone disembarked from the streetcar. They shook out wrinkled skirts. The younger men placed dark hats on dark-haired heads. Dried sleep was cleaned from the corner of a child's eye. They gathered on the sidewalk to decide which way to walk: Hasna and Nasef; Albert and Esene; Safiyah and Amelia and their husbands and children.

"What street are we trying to find, for God's sake?" asked Amelia's husband.

"Hancock Street," answered Safiyah impatiently.

"Here we are then," Esene called out boldly, pointing to a street sign a few yards away.

A simple slip. A flick of the serpent's tongue. Esene's eyes opened wide, beseeching Albert.

"What did you say, Esene?" asked Amelia, slightly out of breath from the exertion of lowering herself from the platform of the streetcar.

"I said," Esene looked at her evenly, " 'Here . . . we . . . are . . . then.' "

"What does she mean, Albert?" asked Safiyah as she joined arms with her husband.

While the children explored the sidewalk ahead of them, Albert's mother, his sisters, their husbands drew sharply toward him. His father, unaware, stood apart, left behind.

"This is the New World," Albert said softly.

"You're responsible for this?" Safiyah asked.

"The cat is out of the bag," said Esene.

The group shifted toward Esene.

"Arabic, too?" Safiyah asked.

"No. Only English."

"Can you write?"

"Yes."

Amelia burst into tears. When Albert looked at his mother, he saw a hint of surprise behind her solid deference. Albert's father, in his old man's sweater, stood holding his lightly crushed brown hat in both hands, uncaring, impassive, waiting to be urged in the right direction by a son-in-law's hands.

"How could you do this? Keep such a secret from your family?"

Albert answered, "Not a secret. A surprise."

It took some time for Albert's family to accustom itself to the sight of Esene's reading whatever came in front of her. When she was silent, they suspected she was reading and looked around the room to determine the object of her attention. After the first set of Christmas cards (Albert had chosen a Madonna and Child), Safiyah and Amelia invited Father Nicholas to Safiyah's prosperous home for coffee and cakes and steered the conversation to the great sin of pride, which caused the downfall of the favorite angel of God.

At Easter, an old woman was called in on the pretext of having lunch. Through her fingers she sifted the sand she'd brought in the broad, flat brass box. "From the old country," she assured them, referring to the sand. Her eyes traveled over the ridges, which she leveled and created again according to a plan Esene didn't divine. "Beware," she finally told Esene, lifting her fortune from the sifting grains, and it was clear from the tone of her voice that it pained her to deliver the message. "The consequences of a life of following your own inclinations are not easy to control."

When the men argued American politics in Arabic and the children who went to American schools played outdoors, the women, including Esene, sat on Hasna's porch on hard-backed chairs carried from the kitchen. If Esene walked past the living room, the men's mouths snapped shut like empty purses. Even Albert's exhortations to Esene to join them did not revive their powers of speech. "They're old-fashioned," Albert would say later. "They're not the beginning and the end." Still, it bored him to sit on the porch with the women. To have to listen to Safiyah say, "You need more lemon in your tabbouleh, Esene." Or to hear Amelia add, "If I were you, I'd increase the cinnamon in the rice," as though a woman who read and had no children could expect nothing else.

The evening of the day she had read that first word out loud before Albert's family, Esene had breathed into his ear, "Oh, Albert, I didn't mean to."

"Our secret—," he began.

"What did you expect?" Esene wailed. "The words became automatic. They were swirling around in front of my eyes, in my head. It was only a matter of time before they flew out my mouth."

After dinner, Albert had walked back to his shop and rearranged everything on the shelves. He smoked. He drank a little whiskey. He sat alone while Esene, remorseful and fearful, read the evening papers. For most of one month he worked late, missing dinner at home. One night, Esene packed food and took it to the grocery.

"Give me a drink," she said, as she unwrapped the food. "You always like the taste of bourbon in my mouth."

The lights in the shop attracted an older man, a regular customer. "Something wrong?" he asked when he reached the door. "No, come in. Talk with us," Albert said in English. Esene listened this night and many of the others. When Albert decided to extend the hours of the shop into the evening, Esene joined him and the small circle of men—never more than four or five—for conversation and coffee. She began coming earlier in the afternoon, carrying their dinner so they didn't have to break away until they finally locked the door.

Albert and Esene grew old. It was his idea that Esene should learn to cook American food, and when he found a cooking class at the local adult school, and when he bought their car, he drove her every evening, reading his newspaper in the front seat while she was inside, and taking her home again when she came out.

It was her idea to get a library card.

"I need to be able to explain why I say what I say," she told Albert.

And so Esene walked stiffly up the imposing steps of the main library downtown and through the majestic double-glass doors and asked the librarian for an application. And in response to the librarian's request, on this day and this day only, Esene wrote in ink.

Albert and Esene continued to send Christmas cards each year. Albert chose them and Esene wrote them at their small kitchen table: salutations, season's greetings, expressions of love from her and Albert, and, more often than not, her opinions on the world in general or certain issues in particular, quotations from favorite articles, wise sayings, bits of advice. All in pencil in her childlike script. Esene, unfinished, yet whole; Albert, quite pleased.

Genevieve

1

Genevieve was a heeler. Cuban heels, high heels, leather heels; heels by the dozen, heels covered with precut pieces of dried snakeskin tied in small bundles with an oily string and packed in a box with directions on the back.

"I love working the black patent," Genevieve said, her thumbs and the ends of her fingers immersed in the shallow pan, stroking the supple, black surface as the acid softened and tamed it. Underneath the heavy gloves, Genevieve's fingertips were cracked and yellowed, like aging rolls of paper.

But not her feet—her perfect, tiny feet. Or her perfect, tiny toes. Like pearls in a velvet box. And her insteps, as sleek and white as a ski slope in the sun and, for some, as blinding.

28

"Where's that girl? Genevieve!"

It was a group of four salesmen, and they wanted Gene-vieve's feet to show off their shoes. Four, because there wasn't enough work to go around and they wanted to stay in circulation and not be home, or meaninglessly dressed in suits on the street, so they spread the potential for suc-cess over as many of them as possible.

"This is what they'll look like when they're finished," said one of them to her boss. After the parts were assem-bled by the cutters, the sewers, the heelers, and the lasters, so called by Genevieve because their job came last: they molded the shoes, giving them integrity and shape.

Genevieve held out her leg and preening foot: a few inches of purple suede on a platform with an open toe, through which shone a cherry nail as polished as a fire en-gine. Each night, Genevieve smoothed her legs and her feet and reviewed her toenails in the conspicuous absence of her secret husband, Salvatore Ruggirello.

By nine o'clock at night, he was polishing off his shift at the catalogue warehouse where, to cover enough territory, he rode the hundreds of yards of cement floors from counter to stack and back again, on roller skates—he and the other men who slid around on wheels for their eight-hour shifts, cigarettes dangling from their lips against all regulations.

Sal was squat and fit and mellow. He rolled his shirt sleeves over biceps that were nothing to be ashamed of. After the warehouse, he'd be a grocer and lose the store and disappear for twenty-four hours to drink alone, wandering the streets where the competition put him out of business, kicking trashcans, and cursing loudly in Italian, although nobody called the police. Then he'd work for one week in his brother-in-law's dry goods store in Mexicali and finally settle into the huge vats at the local brewery, which he cleaned and conditioned for thirty years, until his early retirement. Because of him, his mother-in-law, Hasna, had beer in her refrigerator from the day he took the job until the day she died.

"When are you going to tell your mother we're married, Gen?" Sal asked her again. He was tired of going to the movies every night or the bar down the street. He was sick of his father's living room. He resented having to drive in a borrowed car to one of the canyons in East Los Angeles to be alone with his own wife.

"I can't tell her yet. My dad says it's not a good idea."

"Why do we have to do this?"

"You know why. You're Italian. She wants me to marry a Syrian. I told her I won't. They want to be waited on hand and foot."

And here Genevieve lifted her foot from under the table and set it against Sal's thigh, which rested against the seat of his chair.

"Besides, Sal, she's sick."

"She's only sick because she wants you to stay home."

"I'll tell her as soon as I can, Sal."

"When?"

"Maybe tomorrow. She goes to the doctor. Let's see what he says."

"Why don't you have your dad tell her?"

"He's afraid."

"But he was glad when you told him?"

"He said, 'Fine, fine.' "

"You think he's glad?"

"Sure, I think he's glad."

"Ask him tomorrow if he's glad."

"I'll ask him tonight after my mother's asleep."

"Ask him tomorrow at the factory. He'll be in a better mood."

They were finished with their beer and wine and scraped the metal tips of their chair legs against the linoleum, the last to leave except for the owner's children, who played on the sawdust floor.

The next day, Genevieve made a point of finding her father before lunch. Behind him a wall of finished shoes rose like the side of a mountain to the sky. The old man rode a wooden ladder from one side to the other, gathering an armful of white leather pumps that looked like swans brought in from a storm. With his own formulas and se-cret solutions, he erased the fingerprints and smudges that remained on the finished shoes, the final step before packaging.

"Joe works miracles," the boss said, which is why he hired Joe's daughter when she came looking for work. Genevieve had been working at the shoe factory for four-teen months; her father, for fourteen years.

"Dad," Genevieve said, "Sal wonders if you're glad we got married."

"If it makes you happy."

"He wonders, can we tell Ma yet?"

Her father calmly mixed the pastel liquids in the heavy glass trays and said, "Let's wait a little longer."

2

Every morning, Hasna swept her house, the final leg of her broom's journey ending at the front door in time for the senior Mr. Ruggirello—Mario, Sal's father—to limp by with his cane. When he came to Hasna's walkway, he invariably slowed his pace, so that some mornings he seemed to be limping in place, like a broken windup toy that had hit an obstacle in the road. He never called Hasna's name or turned the right angle toward her door unless he heard her say, "Mario, come in and visit." Or words to that effect.

She'd pour them each a small glass of whiskey and a tall glass of water. Then a second whiskey. And possibly another if the day was cold. In forty-five minutes Mr. Ruggirello would resume his walk. They never talked of their children; they said the same things every day.

Hasna: "How are you feeling?"

Mario: "The same. How about you?"

Hasna: "The same."

Mario: "Joe's at work?"

Hasna: "God willing . . . Your leg's all right?"

Mario: "It's fine."

At this point, they might be joined by the mailman. After Hasna had first granted him a drink, he lingered at the mailbox each morning, making noise by combining and recombining the small delivery of bills and letters from relatives back east, and by kicking the bottom of the screen door so loudly, no person inside, other than an invalid or a drunk, could ignore it. Each time Hasna said, "Mario, shall I invite him in?" And Mario answered, "Sure." The mailman, who was only a couple of years short of retirement himself, joined them at the doily-covered, high mahogany table and Hasna poured him a drink.

"Bottoms up," he said and they all laughed, but Hasna didn't ask him to sit. And she never offered him a second. He'd drink his one drink in a noisy, appreciative gulp, resist wiping his mouth on his sleeve, and leave.

"Nice man," declared Mario.

"Nice man," Hasna agreed.

One evening Genevieve said, "I know you have a drink with Mario Ruggirello every morning."

"A little drink won't hurt me once in a while."

"What would the doctor say if he knew you drank every morning?"

"He knows, but what's he going to do?"

"You shouldn't make yourself sicker on purpose."

"It makes me feel better, not sicker." Genevieve handed her mother a glass of hot water with a floating piece of lemon.

"What do you and Mario talk about?" Genevieve asked.

"Nothing."

"I don't believe you."

"We don't talk about nothing. If you don't believe me, ask him—"

"—I will—"

"—sometime when you're over there. You're over there too much."

"I visit Sal there sometimes after work."

"Why go visit Sal so much?"

"I visit Sal; you visit Mario. What's the difference?"

"We both know the difference."

3

Genevieve's older sister, Angell, mother of four and wife to a rich Syrian in dry goods, lived in Mexicali on the hillside occupied by Americans; Angell's best friend had a ballroom in her house. Angell's husband, Sabeh, kicked the pets, hit his children, slapped his wife. They couldn't escape him because he knew everyone and received deference for his well-known public generosities. One morning, the principal at the English-speaking, American-run school called him at the main store to tell him his children weren't there, and Sabeh rampaged home in time to find the two boys and two girls dressed and standing inside the closed front door—their bulging suitcases behind them—

and Angell racing down the stairs to join them, wearing her favorite peach hat and suit and her glistening French nail polish. Sabeh dismissed the arriving taxi and made Angell's life more miserable than it had been before.

Angell wrote home and begged her family to come visit her. Her mother, unmoved, said, "She should have known." Hasna would not go because, years before, Angell had run away with Sabeh to get married. "She made her bed," Hasna said without softening. Even though Angell insisted it had been more like an abduction: she, fourteen; he, twenty-nine.

But Joe packed boxes of food and bottles of water and found a couch to wedge against the wooden slats of the truck bed and told Genevieve and her younger brother, Leo (since deceased), to climb in back. Joe wanted them to ride in comfort over the desert back roads and through the towns, which were scattered over the sand like animal bones.

The children made jokes about the end of the string Joe had pinned to one arm of the couch. They watched as he ran the string through a slit in the window behind the driver's seat, draped it over his shoulder, and wrapped the other end around a button on his shirt. He told them, "When you have to go, pull." But when that rarity of another car appeared like a mirage on the horizon, Leo instead hurriedly fit himself through a hole in the wooden side and took aim, while Genevieve collapsed in laughter.

Now, twelve years later, Angell and her husband were traveling north. Coming home for a visit. But without the children. Angell said they couldn't miss three weeks of school, but secretly she wanted to see how warmly she'd be welcomed by her mother without the shield of grandchildren. And there was the shadow of a desire to deprive her mother of their company.

Angell insisted on sleeping at her mother's house. It wasn't yet clear where Sabeh would sleep, torn as he was by his competing desires—to keep the trip cheap or show off what he could afford by ordering room-service Scotch for his friends. His father-in-law resented how he treated Angell; his mother-in-law was glad he was rich, but he had married her daughter without her permission and the two canceled each other out.

The afternoon Angell and Sabeh arrived, a small group of friends and family gathered, not including Sal. Genevieve examined her sister carefully for black eyes and twisted wrists and, finding neither, poured drinks all around for everyone except her mother.

"It's not good for you, Ma. Have some bread and kibbe."

"What's the difference," Hasna said stoically. Later, on the pretext of going to the backyard to pick figs for dessert, she downed a shot glass of liquor in the kitchen.

Genevieve had already told Sal that there was no way she could see him that night.

"No more of this, Gen."

"My sister's home. And Sabeh."

"So what? Just tell all of them and get it over with."

"Soon, Sal . . . Not yet."

On their second night in town Angell, elated and energized, drawn to the places she'd missed, pulled the others with her. They went dancing. Dancing. Genevieve's weakness. So, when Angell and Sabeh and their group of seven decided to go, and Angell said, "Come on," and her mother said, "Go, go," and her father didn't seem to mind, she went.

She danced with every man, including her brother-in-law, who held her so close she had to hold in her stomach.

"You shouldn't run around so much," he said.

"What do you know about me?" asked Genevieve, "You just got into town."

The execution of a minor twirl and the whole time Sabeh wanting to smell her dancing sandals of scalloped gold and lick her lavender toes.

"See these heels?" Genevieve asked, kicking back her left foot. "I shaped them. I stretched the lamé tight over them. I smoothed them so there isn't a wrinkle or crease."

"You should get married," Sabeh said.

"Don't worry about me," answered Genevieve.

Sabeh decided, after all, to sleep at his mother-in-law's: Angell and Sabeh and Genevieve all together in Genevieve's room because Genevieve refused to relinquish it, although she gave them her double bed and slept on the three-quarter couch on her side facing the window, her toes dangling over the edge like small clusters of grapes.

Two knocks against the aging glass.

"Gen."

She heard the window rattle and was afraid to peek behind the shade.

"Gen!"

"Sal?"

"Where were you tonight?"

"With Angell."

"Come out on the porch."

"I can't."

"What do you mean you can't?"

"I'll wake Angell and Sabeh."

"You're all in there together?"

"I'll explain tomorrow."

"I can't believe Joe is letting you do this."

"He doesn't know. He thinks I'm sleeping in the living room."

"Gen, I'll be on the porch for three minutes and that's all, if you want to see me."

When Sabeh said privately to Genevieve at breakfast, "I dreamed you rode out of the house and down the street with a three-legged man," Genevieve told him, "You keep your dreams to yourself."

The next morning, Joseph and Genevieve took Hasna to the doctor.

"What's the matter with her?" Sabeh asked.

"Too much sugar in the blood."

"She shouldn't drink," said Angell.

"I know," said Genevieve. "Try to tell her."

4

And so it went and in a few days a routine emerged: Sabeh leaving the house early on business; Angell shopping after a morning warily spent alone with her mother; Genevieve and her father at the shoe factory; Hasna and Mr. Rugirello with their daily visit. Sal and the mailman—outside, out of mind, out of sorts.

Sal knew they danced and drank and played cards at night. Had people in, went to clubs on Sunset Boulevard or North Broadway. He knew Sabeh and Angell and Genevieve slept within the same four walls.

"He snores," Genevieve told him when he met her during one of her breaks at the shoe factory. "He gets drunk and goes to sleep. And then he snores. All night. Sometimes he snores so much Angell gets disgusted and goes to the couch in the living room."

"And leaves you and Sabeh in there alone? What the hell are you saying?"

"It's my room is what I'm saying. I can't leave the house to get married—"

"—We're already married, Gen—"

"—I know, Sal, I said it for the sake of argument—"

"—I don't want to argue with you," he pleaded.

"Sal, I'd rather be with you, baby"—and here she extended her roughened, discolored hand and rubbed it against his smooth cheek—"but it's my room and if I can't leave it, I might as well sleep in it."

"What about Angell?"

"She doesn't care where Sabeh sleeps. She doesn't care if he never wakes up."

"Gen, I'm not going to live like this much longer. You'd better decide what you want."

"Where would we live, Sal?"

"At my house."

"With your father?"

"Why not?"

"Your father. My mother. One's not much better than the other."

5

The next evening, Genevieve and Angell and Sabeh and some of their friends strolled along the cement sidewalks toward a local club. Their gabardines and silks rustled as they moved. They smelled of rose water and lime and their olive-skinned faces glistened in expectation, an occasional dark mole rising like an island to eroticize a chin or the corner of an eye. Hasna had nodded good-bye without removing from her mouth the small, white porcelain pipe that had been in her family for three generations.

This time Genevieve went less eagerly. She missed Sal and knew his patience was wearing thin. But the promise of Sabeh's endless supply of money, and the sultry way he ordered her drinks first and broke a piece of his bread for her to taste, made it hard to refuse.

Angell and an old friend led the group down the sidewalk. Genevieve and Sabeh talked intently at the back. She forgot he snored and shoved her sister. She forgot her resentment at their invasion of her room, her fury toward her mother for not being able to leave it. He told her about his business.

"Oh?"

He described Mexicali.

"That's not the way I remember it."

"You were a little girl when you were there. You're a woman now."

She was so transfixed by Sabeh that when the group stopped walking ahead of them, she at first failed to comprehend the reason.

"My God, little Sal, is that you? Grownup?" cried Angell. "And what are you doing on those roller skates?"

With his skates on, Sal was as tall as Sabeh; with or without them, he was fifteen years younger. Sabeh, introduced, looked bored.

"Little Sal," Angell kept laughing, "I just can't believe it."

"For God's sake, Angell, can't believe what?" snapped Genevieve.

At three o'clock that morning, on her front porch, Genevieve tried to explain. "My father says we can tell her as soon as Angell's gone."

"You act like you're enjoying yourself."

"Why should I act miserable? She's my sister and I haven't seen her in years. My father says don't ruin her first visit home. Don't ruin it for my mother."

"Your mother never missed Angell."

"Well, she will after she leaves this time."

After that, Sal sat outside Genevieve's bedroom window from the time the lights went out until he felt sure Sabeh was asleep. The evenings were cold and Sal wore his jacket. He came over on his skates after finishing the late shift at the store.

"Keep pouring him drinks," Sal had told her, which she did.

Inside they played cards as Genevieve offered Sabeh eight-ounce tumblers of straight whiskey. He drank them without missing the flick of an ash from his Mexican cigar. After winning enough hands to irritate everyone at the table, Sabeh rose unsteadily and walked into the bedroom. His eyeballs were still as glass. Then he dropped on the bed, deadweight, face down on the pillow. And woke in the morning fully dressed except for his hard-soled shoes, which Angell had removed so they wouldn't get polish on the sheets.

When Genevieve went to her couch, she lifted the curtain and smiled to Sal, who sat outside on the grass waiting for her signal.

"Good night, Sal," she whispered.

"Is Sabeh asleep?"

"Snoring like a stuffed pig."

"You didn't think he was a pig the other night on the sidewalk."

"Are you still talking about that?"

"Come with me now."

"Only three more days."

6

Having reconciled as much as they could, and that was enough for both of them, Hasna and Angell talked of another visit. In the spring, they decided. Or maybe the fall. Joe nodded knowingly to his wife. The visit drew to an end.

"What else to do, but have a party?" Genevieve said.

"For going away," Hasna said.

"For Angell and Sabeh," said Joe.

So Hasna cooked: kibbe, tabbouleh, grape leaves, hummus, spinach pies. She rolled and flattened dough, using her wooden kitchen floor as a giant breadboard. On her knees in the kitchen, back and forth between oven and table.

Genevieve said, "Ma, I want to invite Sal."

Hasna said, "Sabeh's friends are coming. Syrian boys."

Genevieve rolled up the carpet, set out the cards, organized the bar. She set their favorite records beside the machine. And despite her resentment that her husband remained locked outside, despite the compromising position in which she found herself, she decided there was no good reason she should not wear—on this once in a lifetime night, this night before her sister returned to her faraway home—her blue satin high heels with the tiny gold disks scattered like confetti on the straps.

She'd been saving these for something special. She removed them from their privileged spot in her closet. Inhaled the residue of her father's special formulas. Slipped them on her feet. She wore her dress with the discreetly revealing neckline. And gold at her ears. Another whisper of gold around her left ankle.

She—they, every one of the twenty or so present, except Hasna—danced. Even Joe: lovingly and kindly with each daughter; once by himself. Although the evening progressed without the pairing of Genevieve that Hasna desired. Genevieve, unattached and vivacious, dancing with every man who asked, whisking one or two on the floor herself. Still, she told her father as they fox-trotted out of rhythm to the song on the record, "This is the last night, Dad. My last night."

Angell poured drinks for herself and her mother. The old mahogany table between their chairs held their glasses, the bottle, and a decanter of water on a polished brass tray. Hasna had promised to visit Mexicali and Sabeh said he didn't mind. Angell glowed. Hasna sat, solid and stoic, her opaque stockings rolled and knotted neatly below her swollen knees.

7

When the party was over, Genevieve retreated gratefully to her couch. She lay flat on her back and closed her eyes. She pulled the crocheted blanket over her shoulders, leaving her fastidiously groomed toes peeking out the bottom. The room revolved slowly. The house was silent and clean. In her life, Hasna had never gone to bed in a dirty house and she'd herded Genevieve and Angell through the rooms to put away the food, bag the empty bottles, empty ashtrays, run the dust cloths over furniture and dust mops over floors and the carpet sweeper over the unfolded rug.

"Ma, it's clean. Nobody stepped on it."

The smell of cigars remained, so Hasna doused the glass ashtrays with ammonia and sprayed lemon water in the air.

"Ma, come on."

Hasna glared. Her daughters, reeling from the whiskey, the smoke, the ammonia, continued to clean. They dried dishes and put them away. They scrubbed the sink. They collapsed in bed as Hasna smoked her evening pipe. Joe and Sabeh had retired when the last guest said good-bye.

Now, as Genevieve finally slept, on the far side of the room, Sabeh stirred. He dreamed of gallons of water pouring down his whiskeyed throat. He dreamed of the gold-plated fixtures in the bathroom adjoining his bedroom in Mexicali. His beloved faucet with a gilded fish tail for "hot" and another one for "cold" and the entire mermaid herself as the conduit for the purified water that flowed through her hybrid body and out her generous mouth.

Sabeh thrust his share of the covers over Angell and stood, eyes open and asleep. Overheated. Damp. He removed his outer clothes and dropped them in a pile on the floor. Stumbling slightly, he headed in Genevieve's direction, his silk shorts and bare chest glowing in the humid night.

"Ach!" One big toe against the post of the bed, slowing his cumbersome pace. Still, no one woke, not even Sabeh. When he arrived at the side of the couch where Genevieve slept soundly, he continued to propel himself forward, toward the mermaid and her moisture and the cessation of his immense thirst. Then, by accident.

Like a ton of bricks.

Heavy, immobile, suffocating.

Sabeh landed.

On top of Genevieve.

Her arms and legs pinned flat, she couldn't poke or prod him. Couldn't kick him away.

"Sabeh, what are you doing?" She spoke intensely, but quietly. "Sabeh, stop it. Get up. Get off."

Sabeh struggled to wake, uncertain where he was, who he was with, thought how new she smelled, how fresh, how young. The thrill was back. He began to lower his silk shorts.

"For God's sake, Sabeh, stop it!" Genevieve said as loud as she could with such a small supply of air.

But it was loud enough to wake Sal, who slept outside,

his head against the side of the house. Who'd come directly from work and who endured the sounds of the party from the outside and who couldn't get his sleeping Genevieve's attention, no matter how pointedly he tapped on the window.

Sal was electrified. He stood. Wanting to smash the window but stopped by the prospect of flying glass. He raced around the corner of the house to the porch and slowly mounted the steps—carefully pointing his feet sideways so he wouldn't slide back and fall.

At the top of the steps, he skated furiously to the front door, which Hasna never locked (mainly to shame Joseph for being so poor they had nothing worth stealing), and rolled loudly over the uncarpeted floor toward Genevieve's room.

"Gen!" he called like a madman.

He shoved open her door. Then pushed off with his right foot, shooting forward like a man out of a cannon, into the pile of elegant clothes on the floor, which tangled around his wheels, stopping him at the bottom. Though not at the top.

In those few seconds during which he wildly circled his arms in an attempt to stabilize his upper body, Angell, roused by the noise, sat up in bed, just in time for his right elbow to clip her under the chin before the rest of him came to a halt. It was a miracle, they all agreed later, he didn't break her neck.

Poor Joe. Tossed out of bed by the cries of both his daughters, as though it wasn't enough that twice a night he put up with the comings and goings of the freight train a half mile down the street. As though it wasn't enough that his wife said she was sick whenever he glanced below her waist. As though he hadn't lost his little Leo when the boy was finally big enough to come to the factory and see the boss shake Joe's hand and marvel about his way with shoes.

"I'm coming! I'm coming!"

The floor was cool under Joe's troubled feet. He slid his left hand over the wall inside Genevieve's door and switched on the light, while his right arm menaced with the fire poker he'd grabbed on his way.

Poor Joe.

Confronted with that configuration of bodies under the glaring ceiling light.

After they got Sabeh, still drunk, back in bed, Genevieve told her sister of her marriage to Sal. Sal apologized to Angell for the bruise on her chin, among other things. Joe went back to his room, where Hasna, unperturbed and uninformed, slept soundly.

When Sabeh and Angell left for Mexicali the next day, Sal came over to say good-bye.

"Sal, did you meet Sabeh?" Hasna asked, eyeing the two men, making comparisons.

That night, Genevieve packed her belongings in four brown paper shopping bags. In one of them, heels and straps, open toes and curved insteps surged toward the brim. When her parents were asleep, she opened her window and smiled radiantly at Sal, who was waiting for her outside.

"How can I carry four bags at once, Gen?"

"For God's sake, don't complain now," she said before she lifted her legs over the windowsill and dropped to the ground.

It was the way she'd always planned on leaving.

When she and Sal returned a week later, bringing with them six bags—Genevieve's four and two for Sal—as well as Sal's dresser and his console radio, they used the front door. The things that no longer fit in Genevieve's room were moved to Mr. Rugirello's house. Mr. Rugirello joked it was an even trade.

The War

In 1943, Freddy Simon went to war, leaving Nora behind at home. Home was the house of her mother-in-law. Her father-in-law, his interests removed from domesticity, barely made an imprint, barely had a claim to the premises. The house belonged to Situe.

Nora tiptoed through Situe's house like a bad child awaiting discovery. She never touched; she never made a mess. She did the dishes from the evening meal. Her room, which she shared with the baby, contained a double bed, a crib, two dressers covered with pictures from the old country, a large wooden chest, three armchairs and lace curtains at the windows. It was so crowded that Nora couldn't hold the baby and turn around at the same time, but it felt like an abandoned warehouse. It echoed with her loneliness. It reverberated with the absence of her husband.

There were two primary bones of contention between Nora and Situe: one, how Nora took care of the baby; and two, how Nora didn't take care of the baby. Situe wouldn't have a babysitter inside her house. And she wouldn't watch the baby herself.

So Nora did the only thing she could think of to do. After plunking the baby onto the mattress in her white wood crib and closing the door before the crying subsided, she'd slip out the front to cry herself—on the shoulder of the third bone of contention. Anthony Chiarelli. Her husband's best friend.

"4-F," Situe muttered like a curse when she heard his name.

"He's deaf in one ear," Nora defended every time.

"He's deaf because his father—God bless him—had to hit him on the side of the head to make him listen."

On the steps of the porch of the small house Anthony shared with his mother, he and Nora talked into the nights. About how she was tired all the time. About how she couldn't get used to Syrian food; how she wished her father-in-law, who seemed to like her, was around more. When the subject of the baby came up, Nora stiffened or sighed. And sank like a boat filled with water.

❖   ❖   ❖

Nora should have known. It wasn't as though she hadn't been warned. After she and Freddy met at the Army base where he was stationed and she worked as a file clerk, they confided in each other about their lives, and when she asked about his mother, he admitted he had one. And that was all.

Nora took him to meet *her* family the same day she told them she and Freddy were getting married. She was pretty sure they wouldn't like him because he was Syrian and on the map it looked like Syria might be in Africa. She saw no reason to put him through the ordeal of gradual familiarity when the end result would be the same: the four of them at dinner in a restaurant to celebrate the marriage—her father cursing Abraham Lincoln for freeing the slaves; her mother, stone-faced and sober.

And so they were married. And after a two-day honeymoon in a friend's borrowed apartment, Freddy loaded Nora, awakened and pregnant, onto a train for a three-day journey west to his family in California. Before dawn one morning, somewhere in the wilderness of Wyoming, Nora and the other passengers awoke to the joyous announcement that the war was officially over.

❖ ❖ ❖

In the current fashion, Nora fed the baby every four hours. Not in between. Always on time. And neither more nor less.

"It's the modern way," she explained to Situe. But Situe fretted over the tiny, accusing red face. The accelerating sobs. Behind Nora's back she added cereal to the baby's bottle, and as the baby's stomach filled and grew, so did the stretches between cries. Proof, thought Nora, that her theory worked; proof, Situe said to her husband, that she knew best, as Jidue, afloat in the adventures of *Scheherazade*, deafly turned another page.

In the lulls offered by the baby's silence, the site of the next encounter emerged: the ruins of the umbilical cord— that smidgen, bit, dab which resisted removal.

Nora dabbed hourly with alcohol; Situe eye-dropped olive oil on the half-hour.

Nora.

Situe.

Nora.

Situe.

"It's still there."

"It's fine."

"I'd better call the doctor—"

"Leave it alone."

When the little stub finally shriveled and detached, Nora found it stuck to the inside of the baby's nightgown. She held it up like a trophy for Situe to see and set it aside to be enclosed in her next letter to Freddy. It was the second baby artifact she'd sent. The first—a fuzzy photo taken by Anthony, a blurred close-up of mother and child, which so thrilled Freddy that he smoked a handful of the pink-banded cigars himself and rasped and coughed for a week.

Meanwhile, Nora and Anthony talked into the nights. Lit up underneath the porch light like actors on a stage, they attracted a faithful audience of two: Anthony's mother, perched like a crow in the window, straining to hear their muffled words; and Situe, watching from across the street while Jidue snored.

Nora told Anthony about a dream she'd had where she couldn't find the baby. And when she woke up, she couldn't remember if she really had one, and if she did have one, where she'd put it—

"—Her—," Anthony said.

"That's what I meant."

When it got cold, Anthony wrapped Nora in his jacket. When she returned it, it smelled of lavender.

One night when Nora came in, closing the front door softly and flinching against each creak in the floor, she was startled to see Situe standing in the hallway. In a good dress. Wearing a newly crocheted apron. Her thick, wavy hair pulled back into a formidable bun. And behind her glasses—alert, black eyes.

"Bring the baby into the dining room, Nora."

"Isn't she asleep? Is something the matter?"

"She's awake."

Hastily, Nora carried the baby to Situe, but Situe motioned them to sit at the table. Nora sat on one side; Situe on the other. In the center of the polished wood, a pink receiving blanket, spread out smooth like an altar cloth.

"Put the baby on the blanket."

From the pocket of her apron, Situe withdrew a silver medal and a tin spool of adhesive tape and laid them in front of her. With her strong, veined hands, she separated the baby's clothing. "Three, maybe four, weeks," she said, her face so close to Nora's as they leaned over the baby from opposite sides, that Nora could smell her sweetened breath.

Softly, softly, Situe tapped the baby's navel.

"We want it to be like Freddy's," she chanted as though

she were bestowing a blessing or asking God for a curse. "Freddy's is nice and flat . . . If we don't do it, it will always stick out. You should see Anthony's—"

"—I don't want to see Anthony's—"

"His mother wouldn't do it, and look at the bad luck he's had.

From the beginning, Nora was afraid to remove the tape— afraid she'd hurt the baby and afraid Situe might be right. What if the baby's navel, a rosebud now, blossomed into a full-grown flower? Freddy's *was* nice and flat, barely a ripple under her hand. And she'd be seeing it soon. Freddy was coming home, and in civilian clothes.

For two weeks, the cross of tape held the medal firmly over the baby's navel. Pressure from St. Jude, Patron Saint of Desperate Causes, persuading the flesh to contract, withdraw. The same medal Situe had used on Freddy. The baby appeared unbothered by her new dressing, although Nora's irritation surged whenever she saw it—when she changed the baby's diaper, when she gave the baby a bath. As Situe, biding her time, crocheted in her chair and looked with satisfaction toward the invisible change she was achieving.

"Probably like this today," she said, holding her thumb

and index finger in measurement. "Like this in two days . . . Like this at the end of the week. It works every time. You don't need to do anything, Nora. You don't even need to think about it. It's all taken care of. Just . . . don't . . . touch . . . it."

Nora decided to keep the baby to herself.

She didn't let the baby cry so Situe had no excuse to investigate to see if anything was wrong. She walked the baby, tucked tight in the buggy, for hours around the neighborhood. Sometimes they stayed in their room with the door closed for the entire morning. The baby, propped up on the big bed, bounded by pillows so she wouldn't fall over. As Nora read, dusted, mended, as she gazed out the window and daydreamed.

Nora became aware that the baby's eyes followed her around the room. In return, she studied every motion the baby made. Reading meaning into every gesture: the eccentric pattern of flailing arms, the spectacular display of flying fists and catapulting elbows.

Out of Situe's sight and earshot, Nora risked her own manipulation of the navel's destiny. Having read somewhere that increased blood circulation helped a myriad of ills, she massaged the silken skin around the baby's little stem—around and around with one hand then the other. Mechanically at first. At arm's length, within reach.

She got more than she bargained for. The baby's undivided attention. And smiles. But, she asked Anthony, could this be true? Wasn't the baby too young to smile? Could it be my imagination?

But Nora couldn't deny that the baby watched her. Reached for her. In response to which, one afternoon, Nora spontaneously lifted the baby to her shoulder. Off schedule. Unplanned. Without a glance at the clock on the wall. The baby's cheek against hers; plump, where it had been thin.

Now with Anthony, Nora acted like a person who'd forgotten something.

"What is it?" asked Anthony as her fingers roamed over the buttons on her blouse, the bobby pins in her hair, the hem on her skirt. But Anthony never heard the answer because she'd forgotten to sit next to his good ear.

A few nights later, Nora stayed home. Anthony wasn't surprised. While he argued with his mother about getting married and leaving home as though it were an imminent decision, Nora folded diapers, sterilized bottles, cleaned mineral residues from boiled rubber nipples. And waited for the baby to wake so she could put them all to use.

She read magazines and listened to the baby's tiny breaths. She noticed the new-baby smells—talcum powder, ammonia, the freshness of the laundry soap, the sweetness of good digestion. She traced the fingerprint lines of black hair that swirled the baby's scalp; the soft rounded shoulders. Approved the proportions of legs to arms and torso.

She stretched out on the bed and closed her eyes, expecting to doze for a few minutes and wake with the baby for the late evening feeding. Next to her was the baby's bottle, wrapped in a towel to keep it warm.

Instead, her next sensations were of cold and light. Of stiffness in her neck. Of a shift in the level of background noise.

Morning.

Startled, she sat up.

The baby! Nora leaned over the silent crib. Alive and breathing. Asleep and well. As Nora flushed with the victory of the first night slept through, the baby began to suck the air with hunger. Nora hurried to feed her before she started to cry: the baby's crying always made her hands shake.

She lifted the waking baby's nightgown, exposing the pink, bowlegged knees; patted the bottoms of the tiny feet with the palm of her hand. Lifted the nightgown further up and saw that the medal held secure. She wrapped the baby in the pale green shawl that Situe had made. The baby's arms she left free. Still, no crying. The baby, fully awake now, watched her mother's face.

Nora settled into the pillows on her bed and cradled the baby's head in the crook of her left arm. Gently she nudged the baby's lips apart with the rubber nipple she had meticulously washed and sterilized. She stroked the baby's arm with the back of her left hand. Her fingers whispered over the baby's wrist. She slipped her index finger into the baby's hand.

And the baby held tight.

Freddy returned to a hero's welcome. Local Syrians and nearby neighbors turned out to see him and eat the food Situe had spent three days preparing. The baby wore a new outfit Situe had crocheted. Freddy and Nora learned to be silent at night. When the second baby was three months old and the first stood in her crib and called to her parents, they moved to a new house in a new part of town without sidewalks or grass and with one infant tree in the front yard. Although Nora took the medal of St. Jude with her and used it on her second child, she omitted it on the third and fourth, and no one could tell the difference.

The Table

"You think you were so kind to me," he said.

"You were my brother's child. We took you in."

"I spent a year in the state home before anyone in the family decided to claim me."

"We had nothing then," said the old woman, groping for her handkerchief, its hand-rolled seams intact: her handiwork from the days when she could sew anything she could see—dresses, table linens, men's shirts, dozens of glorious handkerchiefs for the fastidious Arabs who owned the factories or the dry goods stores, or who pushed their way out of Syriatown and into Harvard, where they were regarded as dark-skinned oddities whose fathers were not ambassadors from South America.

"I was a seamstress. You expect too much from me. You always have. You weren't the only one with troubles. When I started, I walked up and down the streets with a tray hung around my neck. Like a cigarette girl," she gave a mocking laugh. "All day I called out, 'Threads? Pins? Needles of all sizes?' "

"You were my father's sister," he insisted. "You and uncle hardly had a choice."

"Then why don't you curse him too? Why only me?" She shrugged as if to shake loose the blame he showered upon her, then turned in the direction of the copper urn half full of thick Arabic coffee.

"Is the coffee ready?"

"Yes."

Deftly, he poured the coffee into porcelain mugs, guided her hand to hers, shaped her fingers around it. Without asking, he dropped two spoonfuls of sugar in her cup and stirred.

"Thank you."

His Auntie Zumirood. The emerald, the jewel. To her husband. To the ladies and gentlemen she served.

"You read our fortunes when we're finished," she commanded. Her lips sought the rim of her cup and she sucked in her coffee. He was elegant by comparison. If she were younger, if she could see, she'd be cuffing his sleeves and bowing like a servant.

She'd place his name among her "accounts of honor" as

she'd called them: those for whom an order of a dozen shirts was so routine they might forget to pick them up on the appointed day. Or her handkerchiefs. She was famous, within the confines of her cinnamon-scented world, for her handkerchiefs. The noses of the rich, she privately congratulated herself or occasionally confided to her husband, blew into her handcrafted squares of fine white linen. If an ignorant maid bleached them into tissue paper or they simply disappeared, one by one, like ungrateful children, she produced their replacements, their hemming squeezed between her other, more complicated orders.

She set her family aside (her daughter and the man before her now—then children). Her husband respected her diligence. And the money she earned. Hidden by the walls of their house, he cooked. He tended. Until the sewing frenzy subsided. And in the aftermath of her pride, a brief tranquility. Rewards and trinkets appeared. A bit of candy. A pot of marshmallow. Perhaps a picnic on the outskirts of town. Every few years, new wool coats and hats—store bought.

And all this without a shingle or sign, as word of Zumirood's skill passed from father to son, mother to daughter, like an Arabic proverb. Her sewing was so fine, in fact, that it united ancient enemies, at least for the distance from the sidewalk to her front door, as the wife of the Patri-arch (in plain, but finely done wool) brushed against the sleeve of a prosperous Muslim merchant.

The door that was opened by the silent, dark-eyed boy, led to a tall, thin house decorated on every surface in every downstairs room by bolts of silk and gabardine. Jumbles of errant threads. Lace dust so fine that a well-placed sneeze caused a tiny blizzard. Customers returning home with stowaway clusters of unmatched lint agreed that this was the only drawback to a visit at Zumirood's.

That, and the sullen boy.

"Don't you remember how to read the grounds?" she prodded, extending her cup in the direction of her nephew. "Have you told the fortunes of your fancy friends? They probably don't know you can do it, do they?" She paused. "That I taught you."

"You're trying to distract me, Auntie. You know I've come for the table."

"It's still in the other room, my boy. No one's keeping you from it. It's yours. Take it."

Without warning, she inverted her cup and unerringly set it on the tray in front of her with a show of force that surprised her nephew and left the grounds, fine as silt, in a small pile near the tray's edge.

"When you're ready," she said and peered into the empty cup, as if to mock him. "It's all here." Her confident hand returned the cup to its upright position. He stared at it, with apparent composure. He nuzzled it with his right hand, but refrained from picking it up. Resisting the seduction. Forbidding his eyes to roam up and down the smeared brown patterns. Refusing her request to translate the smudged hills that coated the inside of the cup like brown felt.

He clicked on a lamp in the darkening room. She stared and said crisply, "Turn on what you please. It doesn't matter to me."

"I'm going to get the table now." And he left her, reposing in the corner of her couch like a worn bed doll thrown hastily across a pillow.

Each time he saw the table, he inspected it like a jeweler, marveling at its beauty. It stood against the wall in the den. He removed the artifacts that rested on its top and placed it in the center of the room, lifting first one side of the rectangular base near the crosspiece, then the other.

"Just put everything on the floor," his aunt called to him belatedly from the other room.

There was dust in every crevice. He cursed the housekeeping of a blind woman. He paid for the services of an ample girl who cleaned her house, and baked Syrian bread for her twice a week and brought her small glass jars of Greek olives and Syrian cheese, which dripped through its white paper wrapper when Auntie lost it in the refrigerator and forgot to eat it.

He'd speak to that girl about the table.

With a snap, he opened his handkerchief and dusted the textured surfaces, his covered hand following each curving leg to its point at the knee. Before him swirled intricate patterns of inlaid cedar and ebony, mother of pearl, woods he couldn't identify.

"Everyone had a table like that in the old country," his aunt called out to him again. "Made by hand. They were cheap then. A few dollars. Today you could get hundreds, maybe thousands, for it."

As he unfolded the top of the table, from checkerboard to green satin card table to backgammon board, his aunt spoke to him from the doorway where she'd moved, silent as smoke.

"Your mother loved backgammon."

He rose from his position on the floor and said, "Let me lead to you your chair, Auntie; the table is in the middle of the floor—"

"—I know my way around my own house—"

"You might bump into it. You could fall."

"No."

She extended her arms like feelers, which recoiled when he touched her, and he watched her find her chair unaided.

"Your uncle took her to the factory to buy that table. It was his wedding present to her. I went along."

"You should have gotten one for yourself."

"I wasn't the one getting married."

Suddenly leaning forward she poked a finger toward a folding chair that leaned against the wall like a stranger waiting to be introduced. "Sit down, boy. Sit down. Use that chair."

Obediently, he opened the chair, sat on it, off balance, as if in punishment, near the center of the room. Like a pair of awkward giants, his waxed shoes burrowed heavily among the objects on the floor. After a moment, during which the chair groaned each time he breathed deeply or shifted, he spoke.

"What did my mother do with the table?"

"She put your picture on it, for one thing. If she found a flower, she'd put that on it, too."

"Did she use it often?"

"You must remember. You were there."

"I was very young. I can only vaguely remember."

"I'm an old woman," she said impatiently, "I don't re-member much myself." Vainly, her right hand pushed at the metal lever on the side of her chair, until her nephew leaned forward and released it. Wordlessly, she tilted back as her feet rose on the vinyl shelf. "Everyone said she was beautiful," she began. "You don't like to hear it, but a few thought she was wild. She had parties when she didn't know how she was going to pay for them. She'd move the table into the center of the room. They played everything. Even poker. Sometimes half into the night. They drank wine. Your mother, too. That's all there is to tell you."

"Did people talk about her?" he asked.

"Do you think they came up to me on the street to tell me stories about your mother?" she said. "I was busy. On the slowest day, I caught maybe a glimpse of the outside. I didn't have time for gossip."

"The first thing I remember, Auntie, when I came to live with you was the table in your living room."

"Where else would it go?" she said without mentioning the images she was recalling at that moment of the boy in the old chair near the table, the boy reading on the floor in front of the table.

"I'd sit by that table as long as I could get away with it," he said, as though reading her mind.

"We always knew where to look you for you," she answered.

"In such a tiny house, you didn't have far to look."

"You could have disappeared if you wanted, or you could have run wild in the streets like some of the others."

In the quiet that followed, their words settled like nightfall, and the old woman's breathing dwindled, so that the rise and fall of her chest measured the width of her silver thimble. Somewhere outside, a piece of lumber fell to the ground, the back of a truck slammed shut, mothers called children to come in.

He watched for some time from his perch in the middle of the room. The table within inches.

"Auntie?" he said quietly, his words ensnaring her, reviving her.

"What? What?" she answered from a receding distance.

"Are you taking all your medicines?"

"Yes. God willing."

"That girl that comes in. She's working out all right?"

"She's slow, but reliable."

"I mean, she takes good care of you?"

"I suppose."

"It's time for me to go," he said softly to the bundle of feathers she had become. "I'm putting everything back the way it was. So you won't fall. Then I'm going. I can't take the table now. I'll get it next time I come."

"Whatever you want," she said, listening to him reposition the table, reset it with her sparse collection of mementos, close up the squeaking chair.

"Can I do anything for you before I leave?"

"Just turn on the television."

"Shall I switch on the light?"

"It makes no difference."

"You'll be all right?"

"Of course."

"I'll see you again in a few months. When I'm coming back through here."

"Good."

He bent over and kissed her withered cheek.

"Just turn it up a little, please, will you, dear?" she asked, patting the hand that rested on her shoulder.

"Of course, Auntie."

"And now you're leaving?"

"Yes. I'm going now."

"Well, I'll see you next time."

"Is there anything you need before I go?"

"No, nothing," and she sighed as if she were going to sleep and lowered her head to one side.

"Auntie?" When she didn't answer, her reached for the television and turned down the volume.

"Turn it up," the old woman commanded, "I can't hear it."

"Sorry," he whispered back. "Good-bye then?"

"Good-bye."

The American Way

Mansour Malouf had a nagging wife. On a presser's salary, she wanted a brocade couch and a chandelier that looked like a shooting star. They already had a daughter with a half-blind eye. Mansour's wife called their daughter "Linda" in defiance of the expectation that the first girl in two generations and the child they never expected would be named after her grandmother, her *situe*, Mansour's mother, who lived and moved in their house like a shadow.

"Why do you come up behind me like that?" snapped Lena to her mother-in-law. The bewildered old woman pushed her open hands into her apron. "I was going to make lunch. For all of us. Mansour will be home soon." Indeed, as she spoke, the city bus roared away from their corner, two houses down. One o'clock on Saturday. In a few minutes, Mansour would walk through the front door, humming the melody from a favorite aria, carrying a folded newspaper under his arm. With him would be Linda. In her hands, ragged necklaces of jacaranda she'd made from the twigs and flowers that littered the summer sidewalk in front of their house.

Linda waited every Saturday for her father to return from his brother's clothing factory where he pressed women's suits into commercial shape. By the time he stepped down from the bus, the only remains of his over-heated morning were the pink blotches in his fair cheeks and his dampened hair, smoothed back.

"*Tameen,* my precious," Mansour said to Linda, as she half skipped to meet him. He always stopped when he saw her, to give her the chance to travel the distance herself, under his approving eye. When she arrived at his side, she looked up for a kiss, and he smiled into her uneven face and wondered whether the clipped eyelashes, which lined her left eye like the blunt-cut bristles of two tiny brushes, would grow back before her next surgery. Together, they traveled the squares of sidewalk, then turned up the walk-way to their front door.

Lena heard her husband and daughter come in. "Man-sour, why are you singing when lunch is almost ready?" she called out. Dutifully, Linda went to the kitchen, where the protein drink her mother daily prepared for her swirled about in the blender. Mansour showered, singing, this time from Puccini. Situe scurried from the stove to the table; the refrigerator to the table; the counter to the table, set-ting out the meal of grilled lamb with onions, Syrian bread and cheese, cucumbers and tomatoes in olive oil and lemon juice and hummus tahini (with garbanzos skinned, mashed and thinned into a dippable consistency that very morning).

The final member of the household waited in bed for his food. Lena's brother, Jimmy. Crippled in a warehouse acci-dent before the war. Elevated in his white hospital bed, like an invalid king on his throne, an elaborate array of bars and rings hanging above him from the ceiling. Linda knew not to enter his room if the sliding wooden door had been pulled shut—even though the only television set in the house was in there, mounted high on the wall directly in her uncle's line of vision, so that when the rest of the fam-ily congregated to watch a show, they looked heavenward, as though waiting for an angel to appear; even though their only other bathroom was tucked in a corner inside. "Your uncle needs his privacy," said her mother. "God knows he's suffered enough." No one knocked, no one called out to Jimmy, no one asked to retrieve a magazine or toy, unless that door was open. Then the room filled with people as naturally as it filled with air. For Jimmy's jokes, his card tricks, his willing ear. Jimmy took all his meals in his bed, on a metal tray that clamped over his lap.

After lunch, Lena called Mansour to the living room.

"This is where I want it to go," she announced as she pointed to a bare pink plaster wall.

"We can't afford it," Mansour answered.

"You say that every time we need something. Linda's last operation—"

"—That was different. I could borrow money from my brother for that. And he'll probably help us again if we need it. But I could never ask him for money for a couch."

"Mansour, we're sliding into squalor. Look around you."

Mansour's eyes told him that his wife exaggerated. From the upright piano in the corner (old and a bargain, yes, but a piano, nonetheless) to the overstuffed chairs, slightly worn; to a large side table (his mother's from the days before she divided her furniture among her children and moved, like a bride without a dowry, into Mansour's house); to a lamp table laden with family pictures; to a solitary couch opposite the wall where Lena stood accusing. If she were a reasonable woman, he'd have pointed out the sturdiness of their furniture, its lineage and dignity.

Lena said, "I found the perfect one downtown."

She left the living room and returned with the kitchen broom in such a short time that Mansour knew the discussion was not over. Vigorously, she swept the baseboards at the bottom of the blank wall and dusted the windowsills, although there was no visible dust, as if preparing a nest for a new arrival.

"I've put a down payment on it, Mansour."

"On what?" he asked with hopeful innocence.

"The couch. One hundred dollars. Nonrefundable. The balance is COD. When we have the money. Unless someone else buys it first."

"How much COD?"

"Thirteen hundred and ninety-nine dollars."

"For one couch? No, Lena. No."

"You always managed to get money before—when we got the piano, when we all went to Las Vegas . . ."

"No."

"Mansour?"

There followed a period of resentful days. Next to his wife in the dark, Mansour noted that each age had its compensations; at least now he didn't burn with a fire that wouldn't let him sleep, reduced to running his finger down the middle of her narrow back or rubbing himself against her covered behind. He thought: how different she is from her brother, Jimmy. She thought: how different Mansour is from *his* brother. Each night they slept leaving a strip of cool sheet between them.

They needed more money than Lena knew. Their extended household could have been supported on a presser's pay, supplemented as it was by occasional contributions from Mansour's brother to assuage the guilt of a wealthy son whose mother didn't live under his roof—could have been, that is, but for Mansour's weakness.

Like his father and grandfather before him, Mansour loved to gamble. Anything would do. The horses, a football pool, the heavyweight championship of the world. His friends would say, "Mansour, here's five dollars for me. Put it on anything Valenzuela's riding . . ." and "You're calling your guy to bet? Ten dollars on New York." They relied on Mansour to make their clusters of small bets, to pick up their winnings and carry their money to pay off their debts. For a few intimates, he managed their small wagers at his sole discretion: win, place, or show; football; the World Series; a technical knockout.

But then Mansour's luck turned.

His sure winners dissolved. The nimble choices at the race track that allowed him an occasional strut around his steamy floor at the factory—gone. The loyal cards that he ruled like a king during lunch hour—turned like traitors against him.

At the moment of Lena's request for a new couch, Mansour was sitting, quite uncomfortably, on a small mountain of lost bets. And being needled for payment. ("Mansour, is that you? You know what this is about. I don't have to remind you, do I? When, Mansour?")

The collector's voice, distorted and threatening, floated in Mansour's dreams. In the mornings, Situe asked him, "Mansour, why are you so pale?" Lena said, "No opera? You must be sick." Thank God, he thought, for Linda, who rubbed his back and played with his thinning hair, side parting it, center parting it, combing it completely forward until he gently dozed.

Finally, Mansour had no choice. He made his way through the cutting rooms to the sewing rooms, past the presser's floor, to the factory offices and his brother's door.

"I don't manufacture money, Mansour," his brother responded to his request." Only women's clothes. And he thought, what a foolish man, he sings opera with the Saturday broadcasts so the whole neighborhood can hear him and he lives with a shrew.

"What does Lena say?"

"She doesn't know."

"Mansour, you surprise me. For the good." He gave him the money. Then he asked, "How did it happen?"

Mansour spoke sadly. "My luck turned."

That night Mansour sat with Jimmy.

"I need more money," Mansour said. They talked into their pasts, their futures, looked quizzically around the details of the room as though the answer lay there.

"My brother was always the smart one," Mansour said.

"Bullshit," answered Jimmy.

Forward and backward they went, over their years of acquaintance, and before that, to when Lena and Jimmy moved into the neighborhood down the street from the Maloufs ("Lena loved it when I sang then"), to the days at the factory, to the few old Syrian men who'd survived their wives and seemed to twinkle, unbothered, like fading stars. Mansour talked about Linda's eyes, the couch, his mother's awkward presence—"though I've never minded having you in this house, Jimmy. Never"—and Lena, Lena, Lena. They turned these problems over and over between them, like dough they were working into shape.

"You need a sideline," said Jimmy as he leaned on his elbow, reaching over to the high table between them for a cigarette.

"Think, Mansour. Everybody knows but you." Mansour looked at him expectantly. "You know the betting world inside and out. Why should you pay someone to take your bets? Why should you make bets for friends and get nothing out of it?" Jimmy paused for his words to take effect. "I'll help you run it from here. I don't have anything to do all day except exercise my goddamn arms. And I'm one-hundred-percent loyal."

Over the next several days, Mansour's resistance began to erode like loose dirt under a steady rain. When Mansour objected, Jimmy insisted: "It's easy money," and "Of course you can handle it," and "Well, what do I know. I'm just a goddamn cripple."

Finally, Mansour said, "What about Lena?"

"Lena? Lena will be grabbing for your pants—excuse me. I know she's my sister, but I know how these things work."

In the middle of the night, each followed his own twisting, thoughtful path. Jimmy, shirtless because of the heat. Sleepless. His hand drifting down under the single white sheet to feel the disembodied presence below his waist, shriveled in every way, it seemed to him. He felt nothing except what he touched with his hand, the reciprocal sensation in limbs and groin, nonexistent. He imagined himself a seducer, stroking an innocent partner, still as death and as cold. He began a midnight rendition of his exercise routine—pullups and lifts, stretches—so that blood surged through his face and neck and arms, his veins protruding like long, slender balloons; his grabs for breath and the jangle of chains muffled by his closed door. When he finished, he collapsed on his pillows.

Mansour, aware that some ordeal was over for Jimmy, closed his eyes in bed next to Lena.

Jimmy lay on his back, his head resting on his folded arms while some of the rings continued their pendulum dance above him.

One morning, Mansour said: "I need money to get started."

"Ask your brother," said Jimmy. "The more money you make, the faster you can pay him back."

"I need a place to collect."

"Ask your brother."

And so Mansour returned to his brother's office, facing a man who regarded him with a mixture of love, impatience, and amusement, until Mansour sputtered out his plan. His brother thought, "A man at last." Then he asked, "What about the competition? Are you making any enemies with this?"

"I'm a little fish. I'm nobody's competition. We'll keep it among the Syrian boys."

"I can think of dozens of men offhand who'll be happy to place an honest bet with an honest man, Mansour." And he reached for his address book, began calling out names: "Abdenour, Abdullah ("He's always at the track," said Mansour), Ayoub, Buttras, Courey, Elias ("He asked me yesterday to handicap a race for him"), Feres, Habib, Halaby, Hitti, Ibrahim, Karma, Khirallah, Malouf. Everything can be worked out."

His brother had a friend who had a nephew at the phone company who could install the phone lines; they'd work out a time for payoffs and collections ("Not at home," Mansour insisted, "Not in front of Linda"). Jimmy would answer the phones during the day, keep most of the books, help keep track of the odds. They adjourned the meeting to Mansour's house.

Lena, upon hearing the front door open, approached the living room like a general. Mansour spoke first: "Lena, look who's here for a visit. Tell my mother we're home." Before descending to her usual tone with Mansour, Lena reconsidered—something in the brothers' joint presence required it—Mansour, energized in a way she didn't yet understand; her brother-in-law, her natural enemy.

Instead, she said, "You must be hungry. I'll get dinner."

"We'll have drinks," said her husband.

Behind the closed sliding door, the planning continued: Mansour, his brother, and Jimmy.

"We need a code word."

"*Keefak*" was discarded from the beginning because everyone said, "*Keefak*," when he answered the phone.

"What about '*burakee*'?"

"Blessing?"

"After all, the money will be a blessing . . . A happier household will be a blessing . . . Giving our friends this useful service will be a blessing."

Burakee. Yes. Definitely the right word.

"But what if I get caught?"

"Mansour," his brother answered. "This country rewards ingenuity. And hard work. I know. I started with nothing. And look where I am now. I seized the opportunity in front of me. Now you do the same. It's the American way."

Within a week, a wire ran from the back of one standard black phone to an outlaw hookup in the backyard. Jimmy could reach the phone without lifting himself up. When he wasn't answering, "*Burakee*," he was reviewing his list of authorized bettors, the gambling events of the week and getting the odds from the local papers.

At first, Jimmy was nervous. *"Burakee,"* he whispered. Anton Abdenour barked into the receiver after his third call in four days, "For Christ's sake, Jimmy, speak up. I can't tell whether it's you or not." This calmed Jimmy down.

Where was Lena during all this? Quivering with shame and pride, the former drying like a dot of water in the sun with each completed phone call. She could hardly stop herself: "More coffee, Mansour?" "What can I bring you, Jimmy?" At night she faced her husband in bed: "Mansour, let me touch you. You touch me . . . here." Lena relaxed as soon as she realized it was going to work. As soon as her cousin who read her fortune in the tea leaves told her, "I see many blessings ahead for you, my lucky Lena."

As for Linda, her father, mother, and grandmother warned her, "You must never, never answer the black phone in Uncle Jimmy's room." When she started to ask why, they countered, "Because it's not for children." Her mother intoned, "Even if it rings and rings and rings and you're home alone, you must not touch it."

At this, Situe snorted to herself: home alone. "Home alone" applied to that short interval between the death of a husband, God bless him, and the date of moving in with a grown child, if you were lucky. Being home alone was the province of crippled uncles or men whose families went to church, but not young girls, or wives or widows. Situe said to Linda, "Don't worry. It won't come up," which the child heard with relief.

The first heart-stopping rings of the phone occurred on Sunday morning before nine o'clock. Uncle Jimmy was in the bathroom, had lifted himself down from his bed to his wheelchair to tend to his daily routine. The sliding wooden door to his room was closed so that the ring of the phone barely seeped through the cracks to the kitchen, where the family ate breakfast.

One ring. Mansour cocked his head. Two rings. Lena stared wildly at him from across the table. Situe—because she was the grandmother and saw herself as the anchor— continued to pour Linda's cereal into a bowl. At three rings, Mansour bolted; he shoved aside the sliding door with such force that the china plates hanging on a nearby wall shook in their elastic hangers.

"Burakee?"

"Burakee."

A baptism by fire, survived.

*   *   *

From the street, the Maloufs' house looked no different. A modest white stucco bungalow with a cement porch stretched across its front. On each end, an ancient marble planter holding an equally ancient jade plant that required neither love nor water to survive. The most curious of the neighbors, however, might have noticed a minor change in Mansour's comings and goings. On Monday nights, after dinner, his brother cruised up to the curb in his midnight blue Chrysler and Mansour left the house, careful to latch the screen door, carrying a small brown satchel. They drove at a stately pace, primarily because Mansour's brother was a very poor driver, cutting wide arcs around corners, allowing impatient seconds to elapse at the change of every light: over the side streets of Boyle Heights and Lincoln Heights to the office at the factory. To settle accounts.

Behind his brother's desk sat Mansour, increasingly jovial as he became less astounded that the operation had come together so well; on the other side, a parade of old friends come to collect or pay out. Mansour's brother occupied a corner of the room, quietly estimating his cut. More than one man there thought—if Mansour has been able to pull this off, mild Mansour—I should have been, too; look at him, smiling and raking it in; Mansour (with the ferocious wife and the half-blind daughter and the crippled brother-in-law) humming opera as he handled the money. Charlie Buttras, George Saleeby, Arthur Boulous, surprised at their desires to be acknowledged by Mansour in a way they never previously imagined.

A hot card game burned in the corner. This in contrast to the built-in temperance of the group. For most of them, their winnings and losses, small amounts of money that flowed regularly in and out of the game, were merely dues in a club. Part of the price of admission. Not counted upon to produce a pot of gold, not the means to a financial hilltop or a dangerous ride to the bottom. The flow of their dollars toward Mansour's satchel was just enough to elevate him, steadily, to the top end of the group without pushing him out of it. The really serious gamblers (and they personally knew of only one, the infamous Harry Shibley, who had no visible means of support and who twenty years before hit it big one day at the track and used all his winnings to buy his wife a house and woke up the next day, broke again)—the big bettors went after bigger bait.

Of course, as Jimmy warned, the problem with a small-time bettor who claimed he knew you as a brother was that he sometimes forgot that he had to bear his own losses. He whined. He cursed. He asked you to forgive his debt. Mansour, inexperienced, and after all, a man who loved opera, absolved one such man, two, three, four times. He thought sympathetically of the man's wife, of the man himself, then crossed him off the list anyway. Later he asked Jimmy, "Do you think he'll make trouble?"

"And lose every friend he has?" Jimmy answered, from what had become his bedtop office, with a new shelf to the left on the wall and teacup hooks screwed in below, on which hung notebooks, lists, pencils on chains.

And yet the specter of trouble hovered over the carnival of phoning and answering and betting, collecting and paying like a ghost at a wedding. One Monday night, a police car drawn to the after-hours activity at the factory—the lights downstairs, the small herd of cars at one end of the loading dock—cruised into the small parking lot, its high beams arrogantly pressing against the milk glass windows.

"Open up. Police."

The taller of the two officers rattled the locked door. The closest man inside admitted them to a room whose silence was parted by the creaking of leather and holsters. Two tall, armed, tow-headed men. Fair-eyed.

"Just a friendly game of cards, officers," Mansour's

brother said. He'd moved to the front, "I'm the owner of this factory. We get together on Monday nights. Just a group of friends."

The satchel, the receipts, the monies had been sucked into crevices before the policemen entered. But the card game, with its scatter of coins and bills, disported itself like an indecent lover before five eager men.

"How about joining us for a hand of poker, officers," laughed Mansour's brother. "For fun."

The officers looked at the table. "You know the laws about gambling? Even playing cards for money among friends, it's illegal. Sometimes the games start innocently enough, but they can grow into something requiring police attention. Do you understand what I mean?"

The policemen looked at Mansour, who sat alone behind the desk. "You don't play?"

"We were just breaking up," said Mansour, refusing to acknowledge their sarcasm. "It's time to go home."

The men stirred, hoping to leave, their dark eyes resting on the intruders—but gently—so as not to provoke. "We speak English here and pay taxes in English and work in English"—their eyes said—"but we're different from you, you sons of bitches, and we want you to get the hell out!"

"Well," one of the policemen began, "everything seems

to be under control here." Before he turned to leave, he said, "Say . . . you guys Italian . . . or what?"

In a few moments the police car glided from the premises, low to the ground, carrying with it the sporadic snaps and crackles of its radio. Inside the office, the men breathed. *"Burakee,"* whispered Mansour.

Burakee.

Lena's couch came packaged and paid for. "No, ma'am. No COD. It's all taken care of. This your anniversary?" She directed the placement of the couch against the wall she had long ago prepared for it. She called to Linda, she called to Situe, to come look. She called her cousin, the fortune-teller, to congratulate her on her vision. She made Mansour's favorite dinner. She washed her hair. She rubbed Mansour's back, his front.

Was it the deep rose of the textured brocade that so stirred her? The wooden lion paws on either side of the front? Or the ebony coffee table she intended to ask for next? No matter. The couple's mutual pleasure suffused the house. In deference to the couch that had brought a smile to her daughter-in-law's face, Situe caressed its back, its arms with the palest pink crocheted doilies of her own creation.

A series of minor indulgences followed. Glass ballerinas and porcelain birds in a lighted china cabinet in the living room; four gold ashtrays that fit neatly one inside the other; a framed oil painting of Linda with postsurgical eyes. Linda's piano teacher took note of the increasing opulence, and, as soon as it was tasteful, raised her rates.

All this is not to say that the enterprise did not require some adjustments. For one thing, old friends sometimes forgot to use the betting line and called on the home phone, saying, *"Burakee,"* and launching into a jargon that infuriated Lena ("Two on number five in the sixth, H.P."). "They have no manners," Lena protested angrily, in keeping with her sense of her rising position in life. But Mansour said, "Lena, it was your cousin, George Anton. He made a mistake."

A little notebook appeared in the drawer under the family phone. "We're in business, Lena. We don't turn people away. Besides, if they accidentally call on this number, they're probably relatives."

There was also the matter of the Monday night visitors who, because they couldn't stay for the card game (which, after all, would have required them to abandon their posts, to be out of reach of their radio urgencies, leaving unprotected a certain portion of the city), sought other means of participation. They bet, but with different odds. They got paid, whether they won or not. It was good for business; essential for business. Mansour said to Jimmy, "You never know where the ripples will stop when you drop a pebble in a pool."

"They can all go to hell," was Jimmy's reply.

For Lena, her upward progress continued. She became a patron at the church. Thanks were recorded to "Lena and Mansour Malouf" on a tiny brass plaque nailed to a pew. Whereas, before, Lena had hated the patrons, hungering for evidence of listlessness or poverty or dyed hair among them, now, as one herself, she hurried to the dressmaker to commission the creation of four new dresses for church: one for each Sunday of the month.

At about the same time, Situe began to assert herself. Whether it was as the mother of two successful sons or as the former owner of furniture of quality was difficult to ascertain. She probably didn't know herself. What is known is that on the day of the delivery of Lena's couch, one of the servicemen saw Situe's old sideboard, her chairs, the field of elegant inlaid wood picture frames: "Now this is furniture," he raved and called the others to see. He left Lena's new couch in the middle of the room while paying his respects. From then on, Situe dusted with new vigor. Her joy spilled over to the new couch, whose only wooden parts—its feet—shone like polished rocks.

Uncle Jimmy died two years after he took the first bet. It was swift and somehow painless. A blessing, everyone said. One night in his hand wanderings, he felt a lump—either grown so fast he hadn't had time to notice it or, having once been noticed, pushed behind the joyous and distracting screen of taking bets and arguing with bettors and counting the take.

After his death, the family was reluctant to remove his bed. Lena changed the sheets once a week. They watched television in his room next to where he had lain. Finally, the bed was sold to make room for a new Zenith television console, which brought their television viewing to ground level. The hats of Jimmy's favorite teams, which he'd hung on his rack on the wall, were packed in a box and put in the garage.

Burakee. Lena discovered a continuing fondness for Mansour. He had money in the bank. He had the air of a comfortable man. He called the doctor to talk about Linda's eye. He asked where, how much, and said, as soon as possible.

And Linda, beloved and encircled, grew up knowing her father was a bookie, despite the protections of her family.

Mansour? He flinched each month when the phone bills arrived. He still pored over the phone numbers, hoping they wouldn't yield their purpose to an investigating eye. He worried about the occasional heavy breathing, nonspeaking caller who refused to say, "*Burakee*," or anything, yet who called just the same. A siren in the neighborhood jarred him momentarily. He had less time for opera and enjoyed it more.

In their closest moments, Lena and Mansour asked each other what they'd do if their world began to unravel like one of Situe's balls of thread fallen from her lap to the floor as she snored. If a loser's bitterness turned to revenge. If they foolishly betrayed themselves by forgetting to flatter, to pay off. They could take a trip, Mansour suggested. They had family in Chile, Argentina, Australia: descendants of the generations that—like them—explored new worlds and took their chances.

"But, for now," Mansour always concluded, "let's enjoy it, Lena. Let's have a good time. All things come to an end. We'll knock at that door when we come to it."

The Hike to Heart Rock

The idea of a vacation in the mountains evolved over a period of months into a full-fledged rental, sight unseen, of a cabin in Crestline that, we hoped, could house us all. It was natural that we should go together—one grandmother, three aunts (married to three brothers), and seven cousins. It went without saying that our fathers, the uncles, would not stay, would only drive us up and bring us down, possibly visit us on the middle weekend; three dark men in their short-sleeved white shirts in a used sedan, curving up the mountain road.

We took the second cheapest cabin advertised in the paper. I say "we," but I mean that my mother, Olga, decided as she usually did when it came to family matters, flinging aside dissenting opinions with the sureness of a juggler, until the only voices that remained were the ones that agreed with her. Her intensity amused my father.

"Olga," he'd caution her quietly if she got carried away.

In response to which she'd raise her elegant black eyebrows and, for the next few minutes, move through my grandmother's tiny house making amends—a cup of coffee, a shoulder rub, a joke about how she forgot herself sometimes when she started talking.

Every Friday night, we congregated at Situe's: perched on the back steps regardless of weather because there was so little room inside; or sitting solidly on the front porch, which, generously, surprisingly, extended the width of her house. Everyone arrived at Situe's after dinner, although why we ate at home when we ate just as much at her house again later was never discussed. At any time of night or day, Situe could feed an army: always Syrian bread and cheese and olives, kibbe, stuffed grape leaves; sometimes, spinach pies, meat pies, her version of spaghetti. Candy in the glass jar in the living room. Duke cigarettes in a cup on the coffee table. A case of Budweiser claiming a full shelf in her refrigerator.

My family always arrived first. My father drove us fifteen miles from our new house in the new subdivision. Situe, usually stoic, looked relieved each week to see that my mother and my father (Philip) and I and my younger brother and sister had once again successfully escaped from our suburban neighborhood (a place where there were no other Syrians, no sidewalks down which your neighbors strolled—the Shaheens, the Courys, the Thomases—so that you could wave from your porch) and returned safely to hers. Situe thanked God under her breath that my family as a whole had not been punished by way of accident or flat tire for my mother's impudent ambition of wanting a house of her own. Far enough away to make visiting a more formal event.

Aunt Eva and Uncle Assad arrived next. They lived around the corner from Situe. Each week they came late and left early. They had three young children, who seemed to me less interesting than they once were, consumed as I was with the delicious melancholy of being fifteen. Aunt Eva was the only one of my parents' generation to have been born in the old country and had lived in the United States for fifteen years, most of them in Los Angeles like us. Uncle Assad and my father ran a shoe repair business on the side, in addition to their regular jobs.

Last to appear were my Aunt Helen and Uncle George. And, of course, my cousin, Georgie.

Everyone thought Georgie was a mama's boy, but I knew better. He was the same age as I. We were the two oldest cousins, and we escaped from the presence of the others as much as we could. Anytime my grandmother or one of the uncles wanted cigarettes, Georgie and I offered to go to Frank's Market down on Main Street, where Frank would hand them over, grumbling at being asked to sell cigarettes to children. Or we walked around Situe's block again and again, lingering before anything that could reasonably command our attention. Or sat on the bench behind the little shed in back.

I say he was not a mama's boy (although he looked so much like his mother that it was startling—both soft and plump and dark, with a small separation between their two front teeth), because, since we were twelve, he had not acted like one with me.

One warm evening Georgie and I sat in our shorts, alone, on Situe's front porch under the light. We were talking about something when he said, "You have a mole on your inner thigh a few inches above your knee." He pressed my mole with his index finger. "Do you have any more?" I shrugged my shoulders. Another time he said, "Meet me in back of the shed. I want to try something."

What he wanted to try was a kiss. I said I wasn't interested. But I did it anyway, and made a mental note to try it again soon with someone who wasn't soft and damp.

"Don't you open your mouth?" Georgie asked.

"Do you?" I said.

"Sure."

I want to be fair. My mother wasn't the only reason I couldn't launch myself into sexual adventure. I should be honest, too. I'd have blushed and cringed if someone had even said the phrase "sexual adventure" in front of me, much less with reference to me. Yet it hovered beneath my surface like those little white triangles that float to the top of the fortune-telling black ball urging, "Try it," or "You'll see," or "Why not?" I suffered from a lack of opportunity in the broadest sense, distorted through the prism of adolescent uncertainty: too tall, too odd, too foreign-looking, too awkward, too eager. So, even though I hated being with my family, hated being seen with them in public, they constituted my entire social life. If I hadn't gone to Situe's on Friday nights, I'd have gone no place at all.

We met at Situe's one Saturday morning in July and, within two hours, our slow-moving caravan was driving in the mountains. Ear-popping ascents; waves of motion sickness. Spearmint gum and saltine crackers. I watched as the terrain changed from scrub tree to pine forest.

After we'd spiraled upward through lush deposits of trees and ferns and dogwood and wildflowers, with our windows rolled down at my mother's insistence so we could inhale the fragrances ("You too, Michelle," she said to me, and I was so furious at being grouped with my younger brother and sister that from then on I hardly noticed anything more outside); after we'd stopped for directions at a small market at the edge of the road that sold fruit and auto parts, beer and every kind of candy; after my father, the driver of the lead car, signaled out his window with his tanned, muscular arm for the others to pull over, we finally rounded one last curve and arrived at our cabin.

It looked authentic. Real logs. A round-stone chimney. A low wall of the same stones protecting the front. Several seasons of pine needles and leaves covering every inch of its roof and adjoining tennis court.

Yes! A tennis court! Can you imagine our surprise? For sixty-five dollars a week, paid in advance, a tennis court! Why hadn't the newspaper mentioned this? Probably because the cracks were as wide as canyons and filled with pine tree saplings. We didn't care. Nobody played tennis. It was the mere fact of the court that pleased us. My mother's sturdy arguments in favor of this particular cabin vindicated by an unknown and unusable tennis court.

Even Aunt Helen was moved to agree. And I simply loved imagining how I'd weave it into renditions of my summer vacation.

Aunt Eva said, "Olga, looks like you hit a home run." She could just as easily have said, "You were on the money," or "Bull's-eye." I should explain Aunt Eva's speech patterns.

When she first arrived here, she was eager to learn English as fast as possible and she enrolled in an English class at the local adult school. There was a section on American idioms and it stuck; she took a great fancy to the catchy phrases. When she spoke, she wove together standard English, out-of-fashion American expressions, and Arabic; consequently, few people fully understood her, although I thought I did.

I liked Aunt Eva's confident way of plunging into the unfamiliar. She had, however, incurably alienated my mother—my mother, who fairly prided herself on her fine features and delicate figure, the sleek way she put herself together—when she said to her one day, "Olga, you look like something the cat dragged in."

That Aunt Eva said these kinds of things all the time and that my mother was recovering from the flu and did appear rather drawn did not blunt my mother's rage.

There was, of course, no appeal, no recourse, no tribunal for either of them. They were family and they had to get along. Their husbands were in business together; Assad was my father's favorite brother. Nevertheless, my mother tried to get even.

"Look, Philip." She waved Aunt Eva's records of receipts and disbursements before my father's face.

"What? What?" he said.

"Here." She touched one spot on the papers; then another.

"I don't see anything worth fighting about," my father said.

"They're cheating us, a little at a time," my mother insisted.

My father's response was to breathe deeply. Eventually, my mother gave up. Nothing was more important to her than getting along with my father. Not even us. My mother's primary regret about our mountain vacation was, I thought, that he was leaving and we weren't.

My father and my wordless uncles had carried in the suitcases, the food, the supplies. "We won't have a car until the weekend, when the men come up to visit," Aunt Helen offered, as if in apology. One uncle said for all of them, "We'll see. We'll have to see about that."

I didn't care, though. I was fascinated by the cabin. In the living room a bobcat and an eagle on a branch stared silently down, flea-bitten and worn, nibbled by mice around the edges. I rearranged the lamps so light shone on them, hunting and defending. There was a huge stone fireplace. There were spiders and spiderwebs. Dust. Not enough dishes. "No iron," said Situe.

In a matter of moments, Situe began scrubbing the kitchen while Georgie and I, in the exquisite self-centeredness of adolescence, unannounced, left for a walk.

The men had already gone: they wanted to get down the hill before dark. I was sorry to see my father go, although I never could predict whether he would respond to me with affection or with a special new brand of anger that seemed to have developed as I did. Even so, my father kept my mother happy. When he was around, she laughed more. When he left, the beam of attention she shone on him she redirected toward me. But, in changing her receptor, she changed her tone, her approach—from musky and mellow to taskmaster, without a beat in between.

"Michelle."

"Yes."

"Unpack your clothes."

"I did."

"Did you put them away?"

"Yes." (With as much edge to my voice as I dared.)

Then, what was I reading, watch your sister and brother, button up that blouse, what did I think I was doing . . .

I couldn't resist. I brushed my dark hair so it hung over my shoulder, I tossed the bottom curls with my hand. I showed her how I could look if I wanted to. "I don't know why you get so mad," I said.

And so there we were that first evening, a cabin of women alone in bedrooms, and children sleeping in sleeping bags on the floor: Situe, my mother, quiet Aunt Helen, Aunt Eva, Georgie and I and the younger cousins. With two weeks ahead of us in Crestline, California.

"Let's get the lay of the land," Aunt Eva said first thing next morning. Stout-calved in Bermuda shorts and sheer stockings up to her knees, Aunt Eva stomped her solid shoes on the front porch, as if preparing for a race. Which we who accompanied her on this first hike of the vacation learned was her standard outdoor pace. Anyone who tried to pass her encountered her accelerating gallop and a hearty "Hold your horses!" I wouldn't have gone, but my mother decided I needed to relieve some of this dangerous new energy I was accumulating. She, of course, never went. She said she'd stay with the younger children and called it a fair trade-off.

I have a vision of my mother—her thick, dark hair held back by a peach chiffon scarf, her silk kimono (a birthday present from my father) tied with a floppy bow—as she watched our hiking menagerie move out of sight of the cabin. I imagined her sitting next to a window whose panes Situe had recently rendered clear as crystal, sipping hot coffee and reading a book. My imaginings, however, were short-lived: concentrated attention was required to survive the routes Aunt Eva devised. Over rocks, down hills slick with pine needles. "You stopped yourself just in the nick of time," she told me one morning as I went sliding down a small mountain, out of control, kicking up pinecones.

Georgie lurched behind me (with Aunt Helen trailing preposterously, protectively behind him.) That first morning of monarch butterflies and blue jays staring with black sequin eyes, of ferns covered with shards of dew—and of us, racing behind her, inspired Aunt Eva to lead daily hikes. She hummed Arabic songs and exhorted us in Arabic, the tone of her voice sufficient to convey her meaning. It was she who decided we'd undertake what has become for me, at least, a shorthand reference for our trip: the hike to Heart Rock.

There really was a Heart Rock, the clerk at the local post office explained. It was about four miles off the road. A rugged climb for part of the way. It was in a stand of rocks twenty feet high over which trickled a summer waterfall. In late winter and spring, the water cascaded, uninterrupted and noisy. Years of water dropping onto the flat middle rock below had worn a hole, three and a half feet wide, in the shape of a heart. An act of God, the postal clerk said. An act of love, you mean.

Aunt Eva decided we'd make the hike to Heart Rock near the end of our trip, when we'd be in our peak condition; when we, led by her, could "put our best foot forward." We would make the hike toward the end of our second week, Aunt Eva and I (Georgie had silently withdrawn after two outings.)

Of course, we didn't hike every waking minute. Most afternoons, we hopped the ten-cent shuttle to the town and the lake: climbing onto the back of the old truck, getting a good grip on one of the wooden slats on the sides, and planting our feet to withstand the bumps and turns in the mountain roads, as the air whipped across our faces and lashed at our hair. By the middle of the first week, we'd been to the lake three times. By the beginning of the second week, we were going every day, including the Saturday and Sunday after Aunt Helen had called home on Friday, using the pay phone at the market, and returned to tell us that the uncles would not be coming that weekend.

"George said they'll all be working around the house. Or in the yard."

Aunt Eva snorted. My mother said, "Since when?" And later, in the same tone of voice, "Doing what?" We cousins didn't care. We loved the lake.

Lake Gregory. I surveyed it from the terry cloth platform I'd spread evenly over the rocky sand. Lake Gregory. Where for the first time I clearly saw the point of my streamlined body, my perfumed hair. I'd already become bored with my cousin Georgie. Because in every direction around that windy shore in front of the food stands, on top of the floats, were boys. Greased and grander than I'd dreamed. Smelling like pineapples. Tanned and salty from sweat.

I'd bake in the sun until I could tolerate it no more; then I'd stand, carefully pulling down the bottom of my suit in back, reverently pulling my straps up, and preen my way to the water. One quick dip and I was out. I smiled at the same boy I'd been watching for three afternoons. Back on my towel, which I'd managed to locate a good distance from the rest of my family thanks to Aunt Eva ("Let her go, Olga; don't sweat the small stuff"), I stretched out, face down. I was two minutes into conversation, with a deep, teasing voice before I turned over and sat up.

"Old enough," I answered.

"How old is old enough?" he said.

"Seventeen."

"Are you coming to the dance?"

"There's a dance?"

Situe never came to the lake with us. She never left the cabin. "Because of her heart," said my mother. "She shouldn't move around too much at this altitude," added my Aunt Helen. Nevertheless, Situe swept the tennis court every day with a push broom she'd found somewhere. She hauled buckets of water to wash the front walk.

"Situe. Stop. Rest."

One afternoon when all of us trudged up the hill, tired and hot from a day at the lake and in town, we found her sitting in back of the cabin on a splintery lawn chair smoking a cigarette. Her stockings knotted below her knees. A squirrel swirled around the trunk of a nearby tree. "He's my friend," Situe said, always matter-of-fact. "Not possible," we children thought.

Situe said, "Here, Squeaky." She looked up at us. "I named him Squeaky." She clicked her tongue and held a piece of cracker in her open palm. With a little effort, she lowered her hand to the ground. Squeaky raced forward and took the food. My mother said, "You children. Don't touch the squirrels. They can have rabies."

Later that evening, my aunts and my mother talked out of Situe's earshot.

"She looks green."

"It's the altitude."

"Her heart."

"One of the boys should come get her."

"I'll call Assad. Where's the nearest phone?"

"You'll have to take the shuttle."

My mother said, "I'll go. I'll call Philip. He'll come tomorrow."

And so it was decided that my father would come up the mountain the next day on the pretext of missing his family and take his mother home.

The next day was also the day of the dance. Wednesday night. There were signs posted all over town and I didn't see how my mother could ignore them, but she did.

"Where is it?" asked Aunt Eva.

"At the lake," I answered, as my mother pointedly did not look up.

I'd told the boy from the lake—who said he was eighteen and was as golden as a palomino—that I'd be there. The shuttle didn't run past seven o'clock and that's when the dance started. In the morning, I said, "What time is Daddy coming?"

"After work. He'll sleep over and take Situe down tomorrow."

"Does she know?"

"No."

"The dance is tonight, Mother."

"How can you ask me to think of a dance when your grandmother is ill?"

Each day, our hikes had become more daring, more physical. I had a skinned knee, which I displayed like a battle scar, although Aunt Eva remained unscathed. She led me down inclines so steep that footing seemed impossible, made descents standing straight up that sent me to the seat of my pants, struggling and slipping. Nothing was too rugged for her if there was someplace she wanted to reach.

"How can you hike like you do?" I asked.

"I grew up in a village in the mountains."

"As pretty as this?"

"Prettier. Overlooking the sea." Then she said, "We're going like clockwork now. We're ready for the hike to Heart Rock. We'll do it tomorrow."

Later, in front of my mother, Aunt Eva said, "Are you and Georgie going to the dance tonight?"

"It's easy to see you don't have a daughter her age," my mother responded.

I turned to Georgie, giving him my most appealing look because I had ignored him at the lake, and everywhere else for that matter for the past week and a half. I said, "Georgie really wants to go, don't you?" And Georgie, to my great relief, said, "Yes."

At six o'clock my father arrived. I'd taken my shower early. Just in case. I'd told Georgie to stand by. That maybe we'd be lucky. The unerring instincts of a teenage girl had—back home in Los Angeles, before I'd seen the pine trees or the boy at the lake—directed me to pack my most revealing summer dress. It had spaghetti straps and a tight waist. When my mother saw me in it for the first time, she quickly stitched a bolero jacket from the scraps. Why, I wondered, had she chosen this material for me, gotten the pattern, sewn it together, if she didn't want me to wear it? It was lovely and foamy, in lavender and green.

When I came into the living room of the cabin, my father's face lighted up. Then he said, "Why are you wearing that?" I told him about the dance, distracting him momentarily from holding Situe's hand, from asking her in Arabic, how did she feel, telling her she didn't look good, and come on, I'll take you home tomorrow. I went over to my grandmother, too. "Situe, bitue." Just a word game I'd played with her since I was small. "Situe, bitue, are you sick?"

"Maybe," she conceded. She sat so still. Behind her thick glasses, her darkest brown eyes were frozen onyx.

"Why don't you go to bed, Situe?" I asked.

"Yes. Everyone be quiet so Situe can sleep. Let's put you to bed, Ma," my father coaxed.

Then Aunt Eva said, "I don't mind driving Georgie and Michelle to the dance. I'll take your car, Philip." She nodded to my father—her friend, she knew.

"Well," my father began and he looked at my mother. Situe gave a little cough, not deep, just a warning, and I could see I'd been dropped from my father's thoughts.

"Olga," he said anxiously and there was no energy reserved for counterpoint about whether Georgie and I would be allowed to go to the dance. Aunt Eva said, "There's nothing for Georgie and Michelle to do here tonight. I'll drive them."

She was to drive, she was to pick up. Georgie and I climbed into the back seat, leaving her in front alone like a chauffeur. Almost immediately, we drove into pockets of fog, which we'd been told descended without warning like evil spirits this time of year, and we slowed to half the already cautious speed limit.

I thought I would scream with impatience. I could never forgive Aunt Eva, the fog, the distance, anything, if I was too late. If he'd arrived early and gone because he thought I wasn't coming. If he found someone else before I got there. I hadn't thought of Situe since we walked out the cabin door.

"You two stay together," Aunt Eva said when she dropped us off. "There's safety in numbers."

"Thank you, Aunt Eva. Thank you. Thank you."

The first thing I did was remove the bolero jacket. I tucked it behind one of the benches that lined the huge, cement patio, where the dance was to be held. A four-piece band—with amplifying equipment piled up like children's blocks—was beginning to play. Georgie said, "I don't suppose you want to dance with me, do you?"

"No."

We stood against the wall of the concession stand. The band played four more songs, so loud the concrete vibrated beneath us; each song having the capacity to move me to despair or exhilaration. I clutched the small white purse I'd brought, which I was beginning to detest as too ugly, too small, too cheap. Then hated myself for needlessly crushing my new bolero jacket and stashing it where it would probably be stained or torn—and for standing there on display, pathetic, like an unwanted Christmas tree.

Then a hand touched my shoulder.

"I made it . . . Let's dance."

Georgie, nearly immobilized against the wall, gave up watching us after an hour. And when we fled the dance floor and ran fast and high over the sand (like laughing forest deer) toward the lockers and shelters that adorned the tip of the lake, I was counting on him, counting on my cousin, to return the loyalty I had more than once accorded him.

The bench in the shelter was wet from the damp air.

"Well," he said in a smoky voice, "here we are."

"Actually," I whispered, "I'm not quite seventeen."

He said, "Nobody knows you're here. You can do whatever you want. Nobody'll ever know."

"More like fifteen," I said softly.

Those were still the days of seduction. When a girl's wavering voice constituted an invitation to continue. When a boy expected to run a finger along your collarbone, then stop; your arms, then stop.

"You're very mature for your age, Michelle."

My arms, my neck, my face, my back. The zipper that my mother struggled to insert flat into the back of my dress opening without a snag, as she had originally intended.

The next morning, Situe and my father left. Aunt Eva and I had planned our hike to Heart Rock for that day because, the day after, we would be packing and cleaning, and the day after that, leaving.

We left the cabin at eleven o'clock. As usual I trailed behind, over mountain dirt that hadn't felt rain in weeks, that hardly registered our footprints. Through clouds of starving mosquitoes taking to the air as we passed by.

"They prefer cows," Aunt Eva said, "but we're the only game in town."

It was warm and getting warmer. The usual assortment

of lizards darted over rocks, while milky white moths favored the yellow flames at the ends of weed stems.

For about two hours we trekked without incident: I, wrestling with my thoughts on the night before, reliving every word, every touch; Aunt Eva, humming to herself. Once she said, "Good girl, Michelle," for no apparent reason. Steadily, competently, we walked up easy grades. Had the trail not become suddenly steep, had the realities of trying to get over it not pulled me out of my reverie, I could have been unaware of my surroundings for the duration of the hike.

The rocks on either side closed in and we fought for stable footing on the rising path. We pushed ourselves up, scraping our palms. Aunt Eva's hanging canvas bag bounced against her back when she leaned forward. We strained and laughed. Fortunately, before our legs became too tired, the trail flattened out again.

"We'll be proud of ourselves after this," said Aunt Eva. "We'll earn first showers," referring to the vacation rule that the dirtiest among us, regardless of age or status, got the first shower—in deference to the waning water pressure at the cabin. Except for Situe, of course, who was always given first place.

"Aunt Eva," I panted. "I have to sit down. I'm dying of thirst. Did you bring any water?"

"I brought something better." She pulled her bag to the front. "Cucumbers. I learned this in the old country." I doubted her, but I had no choice. I ate two large, juicy cucumbers and felt better. Then a candy bar for quick energy.

We renewed our steady pace. Aunt Eva and I walked side by side along the gully. Aunt Eva's level of exertion recorded only by a thin mustache of perspiration. I was amazed that she never complained about being tired or sore. "This?" she'd say. "A piece of cake."

For some time the path alternated between shade and sun.

"Are you sure we're going the right way?" I asked.

"Keep going. We're the tortoises."

"It was a race between a tortoise and a hare," I said.

"No hares here," she answered.

Then: "Water!"

I ran toward what was simultaneously the beginning of an underground spring (over which we'd been walking, unaware) and the end of the stream that we hoped was the precursor of the waterfall. Of Heart Rock. The water trickled downstream as we traveled up. We moved to one side of the gully to accommodate its thickening ribbon. After a while, the stream was ten feet wide and seven or eight inches deep, moving at its summer speed.

"Do you think I could take a drink from it?" Aunt Eva shook her head, "No."

"Do you think many people have been here before?"

"Yes."

I walked faster now, energized by the water's coolness in the air, the hope that we were close to our destination, the uphill portion of the trip apparently over. At one point because of the indifferent placement of gigantic boulders, the path narrowed and we again walked single file overlooking the stream.

Ahead, a couple approached. The woman first, enormously pregnant; I could hardly take my eyes off her stomach. We barely squeezed by each other. Then a thin man. They said, "Hello," with a foreign accent. The woman said to my aunt, "Eight and a half months." How had she done this hike? Was she crazy? When they were out of sight, my aunt said, "They said it's only another ten minutes."

Finally, we reached the pool of water, surrounded by a grotto of rocks. Down one wrinkled and indented face ran a trickle of water, two or three inches wide, edged and underlaid with a feathery green moss. The shriveled waterfall, the silent waterfall, dropped into the lap of a rock below.

I waded into the pool to examine the rock more closely. So that when later my brother and sister said, "Are you sure you found it?" and my younger cousins asked, "Was it really in the shape of a heart?" I could give my best, my clearest answer. No doubt Georgie would take me aside with more skeptical questions about its dimensions, its origins, its distance from the road, but what he would really be asking was whether we actually saw it. Whether we made it up.

The water in the pool was up to my knees when I spotted a green snake abandon the bank and slither in. "A snake! A snake! Snake!" I screamed and waded to the edge as fast as the water would let me. "Snake!"

What a pleasure to scream and scream. What a pleasure to be rescued by Aunt Eva's calm, firm hand.

We found a dry place that Aunt Eva assured me was snakeless and sat there and had lunch. Afterward, I lay back, while Aunt Eva explored the area above the fall.

Years later, Aunt Eva would gather me in again and ask, "Do you remember the hike to Heart Rock?" I'd say, "Of course." Or my mother would come across an old picture of all of us standing in front of the cabin—its newly washed and stamped down earth the subject of continuing critical comment from the locals who'd stop their trucks to remind us that water was scarce that year—and she'd ask, "Michelle, do you remember this picture?" "Of course," I'd say again. I'd think—that picture was taken right before the dance . . . or after the dance.

I'd had no one to tell about the dance for a number of years afterward. So its memory burned, or smoldered or warmed faintly, like molten rock at the center of the earth, depending on my distance from it.

What came after the hike? The ride home with its attendant minor miseries. More dances. And distances. Away from, toward; farther and closer; the forest, the trees. Events clustering like a stand of pines and, in between, the clearings. And later, when I was tall enough to see more from above (or merely imagined that I could), I'd measure the distances and arrange them, allocating time and feeling to some of them, ignoring others.

I returned to those mountains once as an adult and found the cabin. It wasn't smaller or larger than I'd remembered. It hadn't changed, except for the tennis court, which was gone without a trace—abandoned to a miniature forest of pine trees. Some were already taller than I, others were on their way.

Sustenance

At any time of day or night, Situe could feed an army. She cooked. They came. At lunch, her various sons working around the city, found ways to her house where, like a sphinx, a prophet, an eagle—still and unblinking—Situe sat on the stone corner of her porch and waited. When a car drove up, she went inside and filled the plates and set them on the oilclothed table in the kitchen. On Friday nights, when there were too many people for the table, the dishes were washed and put away by the daughters-in-law while Situe listened to the men argue in the living room and the cousins play outside in the dark.

Every night, Situe said her prayers sitting straight up in bed. In her half house, the tiny side of a tiny duplex. The tick of her windup clock, her only company, slicing away the minutes like a metronome. She usually slept, undisturbed, until dawn. But one night the muted shaking of

125

the front door rattled her awake. Situe guessed it must be three o'clock.

Fearlessly, she stepped into slippers that waited like loyal pets at the foot of her bed. She tied the cord of her wool robe. In a few stout seconds, she arrived at her front door and saw, pressed against a glass pane, the face of her granddaughter, and on the porch, a young man in an anarchy of brown hair.

"Situe, it's Rosemary."

Inside, the girl said, "And this is Dominic."

Dominic barely acknowledged the old woman as he absorbed the layout of the house: one front door into the living room, one door off the kitchen to the back, a hallway, a bathroom, an unenclosed bedroom. He stood on the back porch for a few seconds gauging the height of the wooden fence around the perimeter of the yard.

"I'm sorry we came like this, Situe," Rosemary said.

"Did you eat?" Situe asked.

She produced *cousa, kibbe nayeh,* tabbouleh, Syrian bread. She took her regular seat at the table and scooped some kibbe with a circular loaf and held it out to Dominic.

"Eat. It's good."

They ate in silence. Dominic filled his glass to the brim

with red wine again and again. Rosemary, chewing tenta-
tively with long breaks between bites, finally said, "I want
to tell you something, Situe."

"For Chrissake, Rosemary, shut up."

"We owe her an explanation. We came barging in here
in the middle of the night."

Situe's only comment was a guttural Arabic sound that
seemed to say, go on, I'm listening, although her face had
no expression on it that Dominic could read.

"It's the war," said Rosemary. "We're against it. We—"

"—What she's trying to say is that this country is full of
shit. This country is the enemy. We'll do what we have to
to defeat it."

From the half pack in her apron pocket, Situe produced
a cigarette, then set the pack in the center of the table.
Dominic emptied the second wine bottle directly into his
mouth as Rosemary stacked the empty dishes into a pile.

"You never call your cousins," Situe said.

"I'm busy. At school."

Situe used the bottom of her apron to wipe her face.
Dominic leaned heavily on the table.

"What is that stuff, anyway?" he asked, referring to the
kibbe, a brown paste with flecks of grain.

"Raw lamb," Rosemary answered.

As Dominic bolted from the table and careened down the hall toward the bathroom, Rosemary lifted herself to follow, then sat again.

"You like this boy?" asked Situe.

"I think so."

"What will you feed him? He can't keep down his food."

The news spread like wildfire. The bombing, the destruction. The fear. The rage. As Situe smoked on the front porch and Rosemary slept in her share of her grandmother's bed and Dominic groped for comfort on the living room couch.

For breakfast, Rosemary ate six of Situe's famous biscuits; Dominic walked the borders of the backyard. Rosemary started to take the leftovers to the neighbors, as she had done since the first time she spent the night at her grandmother's, but Dominic grabbed her by the arm. "You want the whole world to know we're here?" It was late morning and time for Situe's programs.

While Dominic smoked in the kitchen, had a beer, flipped on the radio, rechecked the exits, closed the gaps in the lace curtains in the living room, Situe watched television from her special place on the couch as close as possible to the screen. Dominic reached in front of her and switched to the news.

"Situe's watching her programs," said Rosemary.

"Fuck her programs."

It was a picture of desolation. A building disemboweled. Men in uniform combing the warehouse for human remains.

"You told me no one was inside. Dominic, that's what you said."

Situe watched the smoldering ruins with the same tenacity she applied to her programs.

"She doesn't have a clue," said Dominic. Rosemary didn't dare a comment, a direct look at him or her grandmother. Dominic smoked Situe's cigarettes, one after another.

At lunch, Situe made spaghetti with tripe. "For strength," she explained over the chewy meat.

The afternoon ticked away in silence except for the black clock on the kitchen counter. An insistent sentry. Unrelenting in its forward motion; inescapable. Dominic and Rosemary collapsed into themselves in separate rooms. Situe swept the kitchen floor.

At dusk, they automatically convened at the table. There was no dinner there or on the stove.

Situe said, "Once we ate potatoes for a month. Somebody gave Jidue a truckful when they couldn't pay their bill."

She bent over and pulled back the kitchen rug.

"We kept them down there."

"I'd forgotten about that," said Rosemary. There was a metal handle, the outline of a door. With steady strength, Situe lifted the cover.

"The cellar," she announced.

Little wooden steps made for the feet of generations ago descended into the darkness. Situe handed Dominic a flashlight.

"There are spiders everywhere," he said.

She gave him an aerosol can of insecticide, which Dominic sprayed into the abyss. When he finished, Situe emptied it on the plants outside the small kitchen window, on the back steps, and under the sink. The kitchen reeked of poison. Situe left the trapdoor open to the air until, unfed and satisfied, the three of them went to bed.

The next morning, Situe arose early to cook.

When the police arrived, they asked who all the food was for. Situe shrugged and said she wasn't sure, but if they waited, they'd soon know. They asked how long it had been since she'd seen her granddaughter, Rosemary Khoury (which they mispronounced so it rhymed with "bowery"), whether she knew any of Rosemary's friends, her habits, her political feelings. Without answering, Situe excused herself from the living room to stir the soup, turn off the chicken.

When she returned, she set a plate of olives and mild, white Syrian cheese on the coffee table. She invited the men to help themselves and, with an absolving wave of her arm, encouraged them to tour her house. They ended in the kitchen, where the smell of good food cooking failed to mask the smell of death.

"Ants," Situe explained as she opened the cabinet beneath the kitchen sink. *"Imshallah,"* she added, shaking her head.

The men in their quiet suits and pale skin prepared to leave, plate untouched, when two of Situe's sons arrived. One of them was Rosemary's father. He had been questioned earlier at work.

After the men drove off in their unmarked car, Situe and her sons took their places at the table, while Dominic and Rosemary made love among the ruins of spiders and the dust of ancient potatoes, their hums of pleasure muffled by the floor, the rug, the worried eating above.

In the morning, Dominic and Rosemary were gone. On the pillowcase next to her wavy, white hair, Situe found a note folded in fours. The words consumed half the page, but Situe couldn't read anything but her name, which was written on the outside flap.

"S-i-t-u-e."

"Or 'S-i-t-u.' Either way," she used to respond when Rosemary, as a little girl, asked her how to spell it. "It doesn't matter. I know who you mean."

Situe put the note in her apron pocket to wait for the right person to come along to read it to her. Then she went into the kitchen to think about dinner. It was Friday and everyone would come, especially with the recent trouble in the family.

Dry Goods

Three days before the grand opening, they found Uncle Louie's body held upright among the inventory, his fall prevented by pillars of hand-embroidered linens. All imported, nothing but the best—sheets, pillowcases, duvets, tablecloths, napkins—Uncle Louie's groomed head leaving a residue on the fabric.

There was no evidence of foul play. His heart simply stopped beating.

Mrs. Malouf phoned the church from her office at the back of the store and made her requirements clear. For her only son, the fourth of her four children: a vast funeral, the full choir, the choicest time, and a thousand burning candles. All at the new store: Louie's store.

"I can't believe my ears," said the priest.

"Believe them, Nicholas," said Mrs. Malouf.

"What about the body? I mean, Louie?"

"He'll be there, of course."

Later, Father Anton told his assistant, "Poor Louie Malouf died. Mrs. Malouf called to make the arrangements."

"An extraordinary woman," said the younger priest.

"More than extraordinary," Father Anton sighed, "terrifying."

But not to Louie. No one had been terrifying to him. So far as anyone knew, no one had been much to him at all. He'd wandered in an inner landscape without boundary or landmark, connected by a fraying thread to the outside. So the injustice of a son's dying before his mother was tempered by relief.

His sisters agreed. "One of them had to go first. We're lucky it was him."

The store where Louie died was to have been his, organized and operated for him by his mother. Because each of the girls had a store, and it only seemed fair that he should have one, too. Besides, Mrs. Malouf was bored to death with retirement in her new bougainvillea-covered house, and if she spent one more afternoon playing bridge at a dollar a point (although she usually won), she would consume herself from the inside out.

"Louie needs a store," she told her husband, "We never should have sold the first one."

A few months later, and it was almost finished.

Through the construction site Louie wandered, a wan, late-middle-aged man confounding the workers; the spinning teeth of the saw catching his eye, stopping his step; the rolls of waiting wallpaper seducing his finger around their circular tops. He sat empty-faced in the empty chairs. He barely knew his store existed.

Louie's Linens of Lebanon.

A misnomer.

The linens came from everywhere and the family, already once removed, from Mexicali, where they had established the first store, small and packed with merchandise from wooden floor to ceiling. The Malouf brothers and their wives working sixteen hours a day. Their children, helping after school. There wasn't enough room to turn around—only to argue—and it seemed as if the shop would explode from discord, collapsing the work of a generation. So Mitchell and Hasna Malouf left with their share of the cash and a small inventory and drove north.

North, *el Norte,* overflowing the Mexican border like the Colorado River before them, through the vast and unrevealed desert. They got as far as Indio before stopping to spend the night.

The next morning, in sand blowing hard from one naked acre to the next, they raced to their car holding their breath and wearing towels over their heads. Sand in waves broke over their path, obliterating it. Mitchell drove as far as he could on a road that shifted like smoke beneath his wary eyes.

When the storm ended, there was sand in the car and in their clothes, and grit in their teeth. The windshield bore pits and scratches; infant sand dunes rubbed against the tires. Hasna's heels sunk into the shoulder of the road as she stared at the landscape. The silent, dry clarity of the desert stared back.

"This is the place," Hasna said.

They opened their first store on the main street in Palm Springs.

Practically a village then, it was an easy world for Hasna to conquer. As the town flourished, so did the Maloufs. Soon the linen cognoscenti trekked to Malouf's of Palm Springs. Presided over by Mrs. Malouf. Always in black, always exotic, her olive skin that thrived in the desert, matte smooth.

In the tradition of their forbears, she doubled their wealth, and doubled it again. Soon there were Malouf's of Carmel, Malouf's of Pasadena, Malouf's of La Jolla. Mrs. Malouf joined committees and guilds, became a patron of the local arts and servant of God—within reason. Wearing faux Chanel at first; and in a relatively short time, the real thing. Diamond rings bloomed on her fingers like cactus flowers in the spring.

It fell to Mitchell to keep the books and father the children. The three girls, then little Louie.

Almost from the beginning, everyone knew Louie was different. He banged his forehead on the cement porch and wouldn't stop until distracted by the color and taste of his own blood. He didn't talk; he threw himself at the floor. His mother hired a nanny, a psychiatrist, a charlatan who guaranteed results through phonics. Louie amused himself by playing with thread in the shop. His favorites—gold and turquoise. School was out of the question.

"What a beautiful boy," said the customers of the shy shadow who slipped out back to feel the sun on his head. His face was as smooth and still as his brain.

Yet, every year or so Louie thrilled them with a random

comment. Once when the UPS man brought a shipment of hand towels, Louie looked up and said, "Hey, Marty, how about a beer?"

Not merely appropriate, raved his mother, but precocious. How many boys had the poise, the graciousness, to offer a tired delivery man a beer on a day in July in the desert? It was a hundred and nineteen degrees outside; this boy knew what was what. And he had heart.

Then there was the time, closer to his thirteenth year, when—reaching and lunging—he followed his babysitter around the house and knelt before her and finally showed her what was on his mind.

"*Did-ee*, baby," said Mrs. Malouf, "*Did-ee*," while his father swore and struck him across the face.

After that, Mrs. Malouf hired a sturdy young man as Louie's companion. When the time came, he saw to it that Louie went to the barber for a shave every day, although Louie cried and threw the hot towel on the floor. Still, Mrs. Malouf got him everything his sisters had. She bought him a car he couldn't drive, clothes he didn't notice. Everything, except a store. Louie's Linens of Lebanon would have evened the score.

It was the only time Mrs. Malouf had changed the name

of a family store, and it was the only time Mr. Malouf refused to order the sign.

Two days before the funeral, Louie's sisters arrived with
their maids and their suitcases. They'd been coming anyway for the grand opening Louie didn't live to see. Their
children stayed at school. They sat with their parents
around the kitchen table, a huge wheel of ebony and glass,
sipping wine and smoking light cigarettes, as the maids un-
packed their clothes and quietly waited to be called.

"You're really going to do this?" asked one daughter, as
Mrs. Malouf sorted the delivery slips that lay in shallow
piles before her.

"Everything's taken care of."

"What about food?"

"A champagne fountain, hot and cold hors d'oeuvres,
cheese and fruit, crudités, pastries—"

"—I mean, for the family—"

"—kibbe, tabbouleh, the usual. Everything together on
the same table. Everything at the same time. We'll use our
linens, of course." She consolidated the little piles into one.
"I'm overseeing the sewing of the casket lining myself . . .
the color of the inside of an olive. To match his eyes."

"Won't they be closed, Mother?" asked one daughter, as she snuffed out her cigarette and cast a familiar, veiled look to her two sisters.

So much had been accomplished in two days.

Within hours of Louie's untimely death, a second list of invitees, a second set of invitations, with the addition of a black border and a handwritten note to come to the house afterward ("Dear Relatives and Friends—Same time, same place, please have lunch"). Louie had no friends of his own to invite.

When Father Anton learned of Mrs. Malouf's plans, he feared for his soul.

"I'll have to get permission."

"You didn't have to get permission to accept the carpeting at the rectory or the draperies around the altar."

"But . . . this is so unorthodox . . . I need to get permission."

"Then get it."

Late into the night before everyone was to come, Mrs. Malouf walked alone through the store.

She stopped, approving, in the limestone entry where, on the south wall, she'd hung a cross embedded with semiprecious stones. Further inside were the risers for the choir and kneelers for the priests. And bowls of fruit. Potpourri. Wall sconces with amber lights. Ancient chandeliers suspended from the ceiling (the scaled-down version of the thousand candles that the fire chief had forbidden even though Mrs. Malouf had invited him to the opening and given his wife a new set of sheets for their queen-size bed).

A holy water font held favors (small, but tasteful— embroidered tea towels for the women and hand-hemmed handkerchiefs for the men). Linens filled every shelf, every glass-doored cabinet, each piece bearing a price tag, discreetly hidden, with a stated discount in honor of opening day.

But the centerpiece for the occasion was the table. As long and laden as a desert caravan.

To her workers collapsing from overtime, Mrs. Malouf had ordered, "Six inches to the right. No, six inches to the left." A dozen times she examined the tall crystal vases at either end, so finely cut they drew blood from the fingers of those who polished them. She'd personally ordered the flowers. The sprays of flowering trees, branches of figs and budding apples, in homage to the giant arrangements in the entry hall of the Metropolitan Museum of Art, which she'd once visited. Louie had made that trip to New York with her, and together, huddled against the cold, they ferried around the Statue of Liberty, day after day.

Next, she checked for water spots on the silver trays, which she had earlier positioned across the table. She smoothed the runners of intricate Grecian lace, which traversed the table's center. She straightened the folds of the damask tablecloth from the old country so its edges stood firmly on the marble floor. And stepped back, satisfied.

For underneath it all—the flowers, the silver, the lace, the damask, the table—lay Louie, invisible, embalmed. In a carved wooden coffin of his mother's choosing.

The next day was perfect for a funeral or a grand opening. Father Anton, in vestments of black for mourning and green for hope, led the procession of choir members through the front door of Louie's of Lebanon, swinging the censer by its chain and alternating prayers for eternal rest with those for worldly success. He blessed the store in English, and in Arabic asked God to accept the soul of the beloved son of Mitchell and Hasna Malouf, dear Louie, whose life had taken an unfamiliar path toward heaven.

Half the guests wept and the other half marveled at the cultural complexity of the event.

There was no eulogy: there wasn't much to say about

Louie that hadn't already been said. Instead, the choir sang a selection of Mrs. Malouf's favorite hymns, as she stood staidly at one end of the table, head bowed and hands folded.

After the prayers and the music and the procession out the front door, Mrs. Malouf invited everyone to the buffet. To the tiny cream puffs, the brownies, the baklava, around which the children swirled, and to the champagne fountain toward which the adults speedily gravitated.

When pressed, Mrs. Malouf showed one or two special customers the exclusive linen collections in her back room. But mainly, she stayed in position in front of the table.

"Mrs. Malouf is quiet today."

"She's getting older."

"No, it's a soft sell, a new technique."

"Her linens are gorgeous."

"Always have been."

The first list of invitees stayed a tasteful period of time, sampled the food, and left with a favor. The second list prayed for Louie and ate well. They expected to stay late and gossip and divide the leftovers. The relatives from Calexico begrudged Louie's getting the best store after all. The cousins from up north, always quiet, clustered together like grapes, while the Massouds, urbane and as prosperous as the Eliases, stood elegantly empty-handed near the champagne fountain.

When it was time to go, the aunts, uncles, and cousins—led by Mitchell and his oldest daughter—loaded themselves into the limousines lined up in front of the store for the trip to the house, where a second meal awaited. And stories.

"Remember the time he wandered away? He was about twenty, so handsome. A girl brought him back—"

"—Naturally—"

"It wasn't what you think. She wanted a reward."

"Did Hasna give it?"

"Of course. You know how she was about that boy."

Back at the store, Mrs. Malouf checked idly for disheveled merchandise and toothpicks on the floor. "I'll be home later," she'd told her husband. "Don't wait for me."

The last of the risers, the rented chairs—removed, loaded, put away. The extravagant candles dropped in the trash.

"What about the table?" asked one of the men.

"Take it, but be careful. Remember what I said."

Finally, everyone was gone, including the astonished workers from the rental agency who moved the table up

and over Louie's coffin. Mrs. Malouf sank into the uphol-
stered chair whose fabric Louie seemed to love, several
times checking her watch before slipping off to sleep. She
didn't hear the phone ringing repeatedly in her office.

After a while, four men entered through the side door,
which Mrs. Malouf had purposefully left unlocked. The
leader diffidently tapped her on the shoulder to wake
her up.

"You're here," she said.

She led them to the courtyard in back, where the size of
the olive tree in the center belied its age and cost.

"There," she pointed. At the used bricks that had been
patterned into the earth the week before.

Mrs. Malouf went inside, leaving the men to begin.
Using both hands and all her strength, she lifted the top of
Louie's coffin. There he was. Looking nearly the same as
when he was alive, his lack of facial expression barely making a difference in his appearance.

Hasna couldn't remember when she realized that her
son would never know her. She remembered his birth, as he
strongly and impatiently grasped at the air, emerging fist
first, straining her even then with his extra girth. Mitchell's
first words upon seeing his newborn son were, "Will that
black fuzz on his forehead go away?" and Hasna laughed

and said he was born early—he couldn't wait to begin living—and that she hadn't noticed it until he mentioned it, but, yes, it will go away, and Mitchell watched the sheets in the crib and relaxed when he saw the little black smudges that remained when Hasna picked up the baby.

Now Mrs. Malouf looked as intently at Louie as she had when she'd first seen him. As if she could regain the essence that had escaped.

She'd played a game with him when he was a baby. At night, when he was going to sleep, she painted his face: with a feather, her finger, a cotton swab. First, those eyebrows—if she hadn't seen him again for thirty years, she'd have recognized him by those eyebrows, black as velvet. Then, gently, the outline of his eyes. The outline of his mouth, his entire face. A line down the bridge of his nose, broader strokes for the ears . . .

The phone in her office rang again, for the fifth or sixth time.

"Ma'am? We're ready." The call from the patio.

The leader of the four men led her past the others, dirty and sweating, silent and watching, to a coffin-shaped hole.

"It looks fine," she said. "Come inside for the coffin in about five minutes. Take off your shoes first. Put on your clean gloves."

Inside, she made a few final adjustments. A slight re-arrangement of his hair, a smoothing of the coffin lining, with which she was quite pleased. Just before she closed the lid, she held his cool hand.

"Louie, you were always the most beautiful boy in the desert."

A few minutes later and the coffin, on wheels, squeaked over the floor, bumped gently over the door jam, and vibrated again over the patio surface.

"Be careful," Mrs. Malouf commanded.

When the coffin paralleled the hole in the ground, the men attached pulleys to either end and, before going further, looked to Mrs. Malouf for direction.

"Do you want to look again?"

"No."

At the leader's signal, the four lowered the coffin until it disappeared below ground. The loosened ropes were cast aside. Then, shoveling, packing down, smoothing, filling in, as Mrs. Malouf, a few feet back from the flakes of earth that occasionally flew by her, stoically watched.

"I want it to look exactly as it did before. Exactly."

She gave the leader a handful of bills.

"When you're finished and I'm satisfied, I'll give you the balance—five times this amount."

"We'll be finished before sunrise."

"And then you'll disappear. Without a sign of what you've done here. If everything is done right, you get the money. Otherwise, I'll take my chances. I'll have to say something, you know. Maybe that Louie was stolen, that I was tied up . . ."

"Don't worry. It'll be done right."

The local papers all carried the story, of course. Father Anton heard her confession and refused her absolution because she showed no remorse. Mitchell was confused. Her daughters kept their distance. Her relatives? Smug, sympathetic, suspicious. Her customers? Alarmed, but they were ready to be distracted by a new headline, a new story.

Mrs. Malouf herself? After dealing with the police, the press, and her other constituencies, she stayed in bed for three weeks, refusing all company, all consolation.

When she returned to Louie's of Lebanon, business had naturally dropped, but she pulled it up again. In time, she turned it into their most prosperous store. And when she wasn't behind the cash register, or walking the floor, she sat outside in the courtyard under the olive tree, where she seemed to derive limitless comfort. Limitless joy.

Kahlil Gibran

Feet like lead. Knees afire. Hands clamped like vises to the bird's-head top of her cane. This also was true: above that body was a mind, steel-trap strong.

"That you, dear?"

It was a Boston voice that called Boston home from a second-floor apartment, with security, in an old section of Los Angeles.

"Are you there?" Less patient than before. Tired.

She had walked ten minutes for six feet.

"One and three-fifths minute per foot," the teacher in her automatically calculated. Now she stood somewhat shakily at the top of the stairs.

The sky was clear and the sidewalks dry. It was a regular day in the middle of the week. He shouldn't be far and there was no discernible reason for him to be late.

149

As she steadied herself to wait as long as necessary, she heard the wheels of his cart bump over the cement step below. The jangle of keys. The opening of the glass door. Those keys opening the metal cover to the mail boxes. The mail delivered in feathery thuds.

"I've been waiting for you," she called down.

He double-staired up to her and, without looking her in the eye or saying a word, handed her a medium-sized bundle and bounded down again.

The bundle she fixed firmly under her arm, then turned and began her struggle to her door. An inch, a few inches at a time.

Once inside her apartment, she lowered herself painfully into her chair and waited for her breathing to return to normal before sorting the envelopes. The "Kahlil Gibran" letters in a pile on her lap. On the floor, everything else. Then she fell asleep, sheltered by her darkened lids and her familiar surroundings—her large teacher's desk by the open window; her typewriter sitting on top of it. And, to the left of the desk, in low shelving from a remodeled library, her telephone directories. For the cities of Boston, New York, Los Angeles, Chicago, Philadelphia. Cities where large Arabic populations resided.

" 'Large' being a relative term, of course," she had offered in her letters to the indifferent clerks in the phone companies, "since only approximately two hundred thousand Christian Arabs constituted the migration to the United States and their reproduction was appropriately moderate, as were their other habits."

In the directories, she searched for "Kahlil Gibran" and all variations thereof—"K. Gibran," "Kahlil" with an "h" and without, "Jibran" with a "J," even a "Kenneth Gibran"—in her mission to educate the Arabic population in the United States on the works of their greatest American writer.

She simply assumed his namesakes, however remote, would be interested.

She sent them copies of the original Kahlil Gibran's poetry, his stories, his essays. Enclosed excerpts of positive literary reviews (with her own comments in the margins in her grandiose script). Often continuing the correspondence long after the namesake lost interest.

And always she signed her letters:

> Lillian Philippa Hitti
> Teacher, Retired
> Boston Unified School District
> Boston, Massachusetts

Lillian Philippa Hitti married George "Bobo" Hitti in a grand ceremony at St. Nicholas Greek Orthodox Cathedral in the greater Boston area. A distant cousin, Bobo played the drums, had a dance band, and appeared in Hollywood movies that called for ethnic musicians—Greek, Italian, Albanian, although never Arabic.

They met in Los Angeles: Lillian, on a cross-country summer vacation, relative-hopping from state to state.

Bobo was playing cards at the time. The stub of a cigar, barely burning, hung out of the side of his mouth.

"How do you do, George?" Lillian enunciated, in crisp, even syllables when they were introduced, as she looked intently into his congenial, beefy face. He didn't get up. Within the hour, Lillian told him she'd been blessed by God from the moment she was born.

Two more trips west and they were engaged. One more trip and the engagement was broken, their relationship "remaining unconsummated, thank you," Lillian said when telling their story.

She returned to Boston and continued to slip Kahlil Gibran into the curriculum of her unsuspecting students, until Bobo came to his senses. The train of her wedding dress stretched ten feet behind her down the aisle and seemed to chug right past him.

❖   ❖   ❖

They settled in Los Angeles because Bobo said that's where the jobs were. Lillian taught school and Bobo worked the clubs. While one slept, the other worked.

Occasionally, Bobo's late hours and fragrant residues were the subject of discussion.

"I have to do it, Lil. It's part of the job."

"I understand, George."

"If I don't flirt a little and give the audience some fun—"

"—You mean the women—"

"—they'll get another band."

"It's fine, George. Fine."

Nevertheless, every few Saturdays Lillian appeared at the club where Bobo was playing. She sat vigilant, at a table near the front, prepared to claim Bobo against any stray woman who dared to approach him. In a black cocktail suit, her black wavy hair tucked under a small, chic black hat, she inhaled deeply from the tip of her cigarette holder. During the band's intermissions, she danced with Bobo to recorded music. She hoped she looked a little like Rosalind Russell.

The young Lillian, the first Arabic woman to teach in the Boston Unified School District, traveled the world. London, Paris, Vienna, Berlin. She belonged to a club of Syrian men and women who met regularly once a month near Harvard Square to discuss their trips. All had graduated from college or were about to: it was a requirement for membership. Although at first Lillian found the men too young or too old, she became more flexible on the subject of age as hers advanced.

The trip to Lebanon was proposed by Lillian's friend Kamilah. They would travel by ship to Naples; take a train to Brindisi; a second ship from there to Alexandria; and, finally, to Beirut, where they would sightsee and visit with relatives in the old country. Many letters went back and forth before they embarked.

From the moment they boarded the ship in Boston, Lillian had a feeling.

"About what?" asked Kamilah.

"I'm not exactly sure, but I'm watching for a sign," Lillian answered. "I'm not superstitious, but our people are . . . intuitive. We Arabs can sense things."

So when she scanned the list of the other passengers in third class and found the name of a Lebanese man, traveling alone, she was exhilarated. Then disappointed. For, she told Kamilah, he wasn't the least bit interesting.

The first-class list yielded another Arabic name—two

men and a woman of the same family. Lillian knocked on their cabin door. A man in an elegant robe answered, and there appeared to be another one exactly like him inside.

"Twins!" Lillian said triumphantly. She and Kamilah danced with them at night and walked on the deck during the day. They played cards, they dined at the captain's table. The twins' mother, pleased to have another woman along who spoke Arabic, accompanied them. Everywhere. At Alexandria, when the twins and their mother said good-bye, it was with the same vigor and sincerity that had marked their time at sea.

Lillian on deck resolutely turned east. She took her meal and her coffee there. After several hours, Kamilah urged her to come inside to rest, to prepare for their own landing.

"I want to watch," Lillian answered.

"There's nothing to see yet," Kamilah said.

"But when there is, I don't want to miss it."

It was midday when the coast of Lebanon came into sight. When the Bay of Beirut evolved into the city, the city into the foothills. When the distant mountains crowned themselves with clouds.

Through the heavy air, Lillian saw ocher, cream, alabaster, limestone, and tile. She inhaled the blended perfumes of sea and land and acknowledged the moist, blue sky. She recognized everything as though she had been there before.

Thus, when the brother of Kamilah's cousin by marriage strode up the gangplank to meet them, Lillian was not surprised that she instantly loved him. And his black and silver hair, and his olive-colored eyes, and his confident bearing. He extended his hand.

"Emil Zennie."

Lillian said she felt faint, which both Emil and Kamilah attributed to the heat and the length of the journey. They'd been traveling for three weeks.

Their first meal in Lebanon was a feast: bread and olives, tabbouleh, kibbe, eggplant, chicken with garlic, dates and figs, cakes and coffee. Kamilah's great aunt had prepared it. The old woman, the sister of Kamilah's maternal grandmother, rejoiced when Kamilah arrived; she held Kamilah's face in her hands, examining it, calling out whose eyes she had, whose nose, satisfying herself that the family line had continued. She said her house was honored by Kamilah's presence. When Auntie embraced Lillian as well, Lillian confided that she'd been blessed by God from the moment she was born.

Relatives and friends arrived to greet the visitors from the New World. Kamilah was quiet and pleased; Lillian, enthusiastic and giddy. They talked of the weeks to come. Emil insisted on meeting them the next morning to drive them around on their first full day in Beirut. That night, all three dreamed provocative dreams.

Ah, Lebanon. Land of enchantment. Ah, Beirut. The center of it all.

Emil guided them through the bustling streets of the city, through the mosaic of church and mosque, of ancient and new, East and West, commerce and culture. Lillian and Kamilah easily shifted to the rhythm of Arabic.

They shopped for cloth and jewelry, bargained for carpets and hammered brass. They bought Auntie huge bags of produce. They visited a factory where furniture was made by hand, its surfaces inlaid with mother of pearl and compositions of cedar, maple, and oak. Lillian bought two nightstands and a small table. She took a photograph of the craftsmen at work and of several pieces of furniture in varying stages of completion.

In the evenings, Emil took them to clubs, restaurants, hotels. For midnight suppers and belly dancers, intense political discussions or soft music. They ate Arabic food and smoked French cigarettes. They danced the fox-trot and the *dubke*. In dining rooms appointed with overstuffed banquettes and huge ivory candles, or on balmy terraces outside under the skies among Arabs speaking Arabic, English, French. Emil wouldn't let them pay for a drink, a dinner, a cup of coffee.

They spent hours at meals. They entertained visitors. The bigger the gathering, the better. Emil introduced them to merchants, professors, priests. He took them to meet his family. He drove them outside Beirut to see an ancient Roman aqueduct and to the grounds of the American University for a picnic. Lillian brought along a volume of Khalil Gibran and read her favorite passages aloud in English. Emil said the Arabic was more beautiful and translated on the spot.

"How do you have time to do all these things with us, Emil?" Lillian asked.

To which Emil answered, "What do we have if we don't have time?"

Two weeks before Lillian and Kamilah were to leave, he took them to Pigeon Grotto, where massive rocks, layered over the centuries, formed cliffs along the seashore and stepping stones, large and small, into the water.

"You'd better change your shoes, Lillian," Emil had

laughed when he saw her feet, "we're not going dancing this time."

But even with her sturdy shoes Lillian remained on the sand, shading her eyes against the sun as she watched Emil and Kamilah climb over the rocks into the shallow sea.

Several times, Emil helped Kamilah from one rock to another; several times they regained a joint balance above the incoming tide. About fifty feet from shore, they reached a large, flat rock, climbed on it and sat, facing the horizon. They rested shoulder to shoulder, although Lillian couldn't tell whether they were actually touching. When they stood, a few minutes later to begin the journey back, Kamilah slipped toward the water out of Emil's reach. Although she managed to stay on the rock, Lillian could see that she was injured. Emil moved quickly toward her. Then the two laboriously returned to shore.

"It's my ankle," Kamilah explained when Lillian reached them. Emil removed Kamilah's shoe and gently held her foot in his hand. Kamilah gasped in pain.

"I don't think it's broken," he said, "but it's a bad sprain."

He insisted on carrying Kamilah to his car and, once at Auntie's, from the car. Auntie piled damask pillows on the end of a couch to support Kamilah's foot, called the doctor, and made strong tea. The doctor wrapped Kamilah's ankle and foot in a tight bandage. He instructed her to keep her foot elevated until the swelling went down and she could walk without pain. He predicted a week, possibly longer.

"And no travel," the doctor said when told of their immediate plans. "No Zahlah."

Zahlah was their next scheduled destination—it was the hometown of Lillian's father and she'd promised him she'd visit. From the beginning, she and Kamilah had planned to spend several days in Zahlah before leaving Lebanon. Arrangements had been made.

"Maybe I can postpone the trip," Lillian said.

"We leave for home the week after next," Kamilah reminded her.

"Perhaps I should just cancel it."

"What will you tell your father?"

On schedule, Emil and Kamilah dropped Lillian at the bus bound for Zahlah. Auntie had packed her a beautiful lunch. As the bus drove off, Lillian experienced a confused longing, a perplexing reluctance. Kamilah waited in the front seat of Emil's car with a jar of coffee and her ankle wrapped in gauze. She and Emil stayed there long after the bus had driven out of sight.

When Lillian returned a week later, the wind had changed. The delicate balance in the air had shifted. Something had slipped through her fingers and she couldn't tell what.

"Emil had to go to Damascus on business," Kamilah explained.

"Is he coming back before we leave?" Lillian asked.

"I don't think so, but he left you a gift."

It was a small framed photograph of Kahlil Gibran. On the card Emil had written:

> Go in safety.
> Go in peace.
> God be with you.
>
> E. Zennie

Once at sea, Lillian wrote letter after letter, only to tear each one up and start again. Kamilah, steadily and quietly, wrote and sealed and wrote and sealed. Both sent fervent thanks to Auntie, although they knew Auntie could neither read nor write. Someone—"Perhaps Emil," Lillian suggested—would read them to her.

Their return trip was different from their initial voyage:

they spoke less, they ate less, they did not seek the company of other passengers.

On their third day out, for no apparent reason, Kamilah began to weep at the dinner table.

"What is it, Kamilah?" Lillian asked.

What it was was that Kamilah missed her husband.

Husband?

Yes.

In Boston?

No.

Somewhere else in Massachusetts?

No.

Is he Lebanese?

Yes.

Do I know him?

Yes. Yes. Yes.

That winter, Lillian contracted pneumonia. That summer, she took courses in French at a small college in New Hampshire. Kamilah wrote to her from Beirut the following Christmas and, for three of the four following Christmases, produced pictures of a new child. Dutifully, Lillian answered. And when she married she sent Kamilah and

Emil a large photograph of her and Bobo in the doorway of the cathedral, as the proud train of her wedding dress flowed behind and around them and down the marble steps like the River Litani.

Several years later, Lillian also sent a photograph of her and Bobo's only child, a daughter named Adele. Adele: with her mother's hair and her father's ease in living. Adele: Lillian's reward for marrying Bobo.

It was Adele who carried her mother's groceries up the apartment stairs every Tuesday and Thursday. And who delivered a bouquet of flowers on Saturday. And who called her mother every day to see if she needed anything. It was Adele who talked her mother into the surgeries.

"Let the doctors fix your knees. Then you can get your mail downstairs by yourself. You can get out and around again."

The day before the surgeries Adele and her husband arrived to take Lillian to the hospital. At the landing at the top of the stairs, Adele's husband lifted Lillian to carry her down to the car. He held her as if she were a baby. But she was stout and wary. Harder to carry than deadweight. She extended her arms slowly outward, as if she were balancing on a tightrope.

"Don't drop me!" she cried. As her back arched, and her legs sank beneath her. As her eyes, bracing against a fall, closed tight.

The operations were a success. By the time she returned to her apartment, she could walk steadily from room to room. Eventually, she was able to walk up and down porch steps, church steps, library steps, doctor steps, dentist steps. She could negotiate her way down the stairs and greet the mailman and carry her mail back up. At the same time, she became slower and slower in sending out and responding to her Kahlil Gibran correspondents.

When she decided to start taking the bus again, she studied the routes from pamphlets she had obtained at the library. "Because I have a lot of territory to cover, dear," she told the librarian.

She identified places to frequent, places to see. The first of her regular stops was Western Avenue, with its long, two-sided line of antique shops and used furniture stores.

"Many years ago I bought three handmade tables in Lebanon," she always began.

Whether the proprietor responded or not, Lillian then described the tables and explained how she came to be in Lebanon to buy them. If the proprietor showed any interest, she presented her photographs of the old furniture factory. Her story invariably included a recounting of the sea voyages, the wonders of Beirut, the sanctity of the Arabic family and the hospitality of the Arabic people. If the stores were empty, she spoke at length. If customers came in, no matter. She waited until they left and continued. It took Lillian about a year to visit each store the first time, and when she was through, she started all over again, allotting extra time to those she felt deserved it.

Lillian and Kamilah had continued to write. In time, Lillian could barely remember what Kamilah looked like, although Emil's face was clear. In her letters, Lillian wrote, in one way or another, of her perfect life. "I have done everything I ever wanted to do," she told Kamilah. "I have had everything I wanted."

Kamilah, in her letters, described the destruction of Beirut, the terrors of war, the misery of neighbors fighting neighbors and invasions from the outside. She described as well the incidents of her daily family life, the graciousness of her friends. She described a country infused with bravery and strength. By then, both women were grandmothers and widows.

In spite of Kamilah's words, Lillian refused to imagine the devastation. When she responded to Kamilah, she omitted all mention of the events in Lebanon; she acknowledged only the Lebanon she had known and experienced. She thanked God that her memories were unspoiled. She thanked God for her good fortune. But she wasn't surprised at His providence.

"You see, dear," she often said, "I was blessed by God from the moment of my birth."

The Honor of Her Presence

Hasna Elias sat alone in the dark, as close to the television set as the couch allowed, the glow of her cigarette moving in and out as she inhaled, exhaled. Watching them draw numbers for the lottery.

"Please God," she prayed, "let it be Nicky."

From the eastern rim of the Ottoman Empire to this. From an undulating village life, where a wild girl rode stallions to the sea, to a small white frame duplex in Alhambra, California. First, to Boston (for only a short time); then, Los Angeles, when it was still a small town. On the train with her husband and children: Joseph (named after his father), Elizabeth, Louise, and Nicholas.

"He's only four," her husband answered the conductor. Nicholas—on his mother's lap, bearing down on her with his perilously large seven-year-old's body. His twitching, hard-soled feet colliding with his mother's narrow ankles, for a second time, a third. Hasna jerked him hard around the waist.

"We don't have to pay a fare for him," Joseph continued loudly, "and he doesn't need his own seat." As soon as the conductor disgustedly turned his back, Joseph raised his arm in warning to his son. This giant, wriggling boy—the youngest, the baby, whom Hasna spoiled and adored.

It was the grownup version of this boy she expected now with his wife and children. Also, her son Joseph; her daughter Louise. Not Elizabeth, who'd been banished out of love.

"Ma, there's no way you can take care of Elizabeth at home," they'd all said. High-strung Elizabeth—she shouted or cried or grabbed on to a laugh and wouldn't let go; she lost her keys, her purse, the days, forgot where she was going, forgot where she'd been.

"So far," the doctor said at first, "You're describing half the human race."

But did they jump over six-foot walls to retrieve a child's lost ball? or call their brothers and sister on the phone every night, all night, to rave over books they were going to write about planes they were going to build from bamboo they were going to grow, cheaply, in Southeast Asia? Where she intended to travel the following week?

"Couldn't she just take medicine?" Hasna had asked.

"No, Ma."

And so, raggedly smiling Elizabeth departed, free of restraints, thinking she was going to the racetrack for the afternoon. How did the neighbors know? Who signaled them to roost on their front porches at the time of her departure, like a row of silent blackbirds?

And, now, Hasna knew, they were coming for her.

Her son Joseph, who lived down the block had begun his purposeful approach to his mother's house without his wife, who rarely joined him in the best of times. Their son, Abe, never went; it bored him, he said.

The others drove their various distances, their arrivals announced by thumps of closing car doors and footfalls on the sidewalk. Up her steps. Onto her porch. Her daughter-in-law's voice saying, "Give your grandmother a kiss when you go in."

(They were dutiful children and did as they were told, claimed a handful of caramels from the candy dish on the table and rushed outside to play under the balmy evening sky.)

Their parents slipped their beer into the refrigerator. Then silently catalogued the decline around them.

The stains and bits of garbage in the sink. The pungent

smells. Evidence of mice. Crumbs and drops of strawberry jam in random patterns on the plastic tablecloth that covered her small dining table. Her floor crackling with outside dirt. And in the bathroom, mildewed towels hanging precariously like rotting fruit.

"She's failing," the eyes of the second generation told each other. Those same eyes delicately downcast as they sought further confirmation for what they already knew: that somewhere in that kitchen or in a closet or under a pillow lurked Hasna's main source of consolation.

She cheered herself in the morning with a jelly glass full. Baking her bread on her knees—spreading her dough on the feebly washed kitchen floor; patting and rolling, taking a gulp, rotating between floor and oven, humming; with bare hands, reaching in to pull out the scorching trays; having another swallow, then another; cooling off her fingers on the front of her apron.

Then a small decanter with lunch, particularly if Mrs. Caputo from down the street, also a lover of red wine, dropped in with a bottle. "Olivia, can you get me some wine?" Hasna often asked, taking the quarters from her black silk coin purse.

In the afternoon, stretched out on her couch, watching her programs, she sipped some more and smoked her cigarettes. Sometimes she sucked at the white china pipe that she brought from the old country.

It was this combination of favorite pleasures which got her into her current trouble. Which lured the sirens and the fire trucks to her street, and her grandson, Abe, from his afternoon nap. From his porch five houses away, he watched the black smoke, like a snake on the Fourth of July, slither under his grandmother's front door and rise into the air.

By the time the neighbors had gotten close enough to get a good look, Hasna's couch rested soggily in her front yard. Abe scratched his stomach under his shirt, turned away, went inside.

"What?" Abe's father shouted at him that night. "You saw it and you didn't do anything? You didn't go over to your grandmother's when her house was on fire?"

"Not the house. The couch."

Joseph's agitation had been building since one of the firemen, innocent and vigorous and concerned, described how he found the old woman a few feet from the burning couch, lying on her back on the floor, her face to the side, her arms crossed peacefully over her chest.

It was the second time Joseph had had to contend with this, and this was the source of some of his fury, and his shove after shove into his son's ribs while his wife cried and shrieked and tugged at his arm.

The first time, on an afternoon two months before, Joseph had dropped in for a visit.

"Ma?"

She usually heard the screen door slam and came out to see who was there. He first saw her feet protruding through the doorway of her bedroom, toes pointing upward as they extended from the floor. She was next to her bed, her swollen ankles masked by thick stockings, her slippers lined up neatly beside her.

"Ma! Ma!"

"What?"

"Ma?"

"Joseph, Sh-h-h . . ."

"What are you doing there?"

"I'm resting."

"Ma, get up."

"Later. Go away."

It was then that he encountered the cemetery under her bed—a dozen or more bottles on their sides, uncapped, finished. The doctor talked to Hasna alone.

"Hasna, why are you doing this?"

"What do you mean?"

"It's not good for you, you know."

"What isn't?"

Later he told the family that everything was under control, he'd talked to her, she'd be all right. He'd given Hasna some pills. Joseph and Louise told their mother how lucky she was to have a doctor like him. Louise hired a nurse to stay with her mother for a week.

All but Nicholas acknowledged the problem.

His wife said, "Nicky, look around. Her house is a mess. She's always sleeping—"

"—She's old—"

"—I knew that's what you'd say. The truth is she drinks too much and she can't take care of herself anymore. For God's sake, Nick, she set the place on fire. Next thing, she'll kill herself."

Every night, Hasna said her prayers. Every night, she dreamed of her dead husband.

"He's lonely," she told Mrs. Caputo. "He wants me to come to him. I told him, maybe soon."

Hasna fished a roll of dollar bills from her apron pocket, licked her thumb, and peeled off four.

"Olivia?"

"I can't, Hasna. Joseph said no. He said it's making you sick."

"I'll ask Tony Sarantino."

Olivia shook her head. Silently, Hasna ran over the names of people on the street she thought she could count on.

Olivia said, "The word's out, Hasna."

Like Hasna herself was soon after. Her home shut down; locked tight. Except when Joseph let the air in, three or four times a week. Her new couch with its slippery and untamed surface, went with her.

There was already a bed in the other place—a chaste, regulation, twin bed—so Hasna's polished mahogany four-poster stayed behind, becoming a retreat for Joseph and, on alternate days, for Abe. Each unaware of the other's occupancy. Plumping up the pillows after a discreet nap. Smoothing the spread. Leaving scents so nearly identical they gave no clue to one that the other had been there.

"This is the best place for you, Ma." (Hasna thought: Elizabeth would have gotten out of here; she'd have jumped over the wall.)

Everyone was there with her. Even Abe—offering a pot of pink azaleas. The couch and an end table lined one side of the small, cool rectangular room; on the opposite side was Hasna's new bed, on which clustered Nicholas and his family. Louise stood in the center of the room.

"It needs a little color, Ma. I'll get you a new spread, maybe in a deep rose or green, to go with the couch."

"Who buys a bedspread to match a couch?" said Hasna.

Louise—whose husband made more money then her brothers combined and who paid for everything her mother needed and, having paid, was criticized for having the money in the first place and throwing it at every problem—said nothing. Later she remarked privately to her husband that it would have been so much easier if Elizabeth hadn't been crazy.

Hasna's first day in the rest home started poorly.

"We're so pleased to have you with us, Mrs. Elias. We won't let you get lonely on us."

(A pause. No answer. A few hopeful looks among Hasna's children.)

"We'll introduce you to all the nice folks here."

(A second silence.)

"Well . . . you settle in now and I'll come back in a little while."

One week later, the voice was saying, "You can't just sit

in here all the time, Mrs. Elias." In the pink quilted robe from Louise, her thick white hair pinned back, uncombed, her fingers marshaling her thread and her crocheting needles, Hasna saying to herself, "That's what you think."

"I was practically a princess once, Nicky."

"I know, Ma."

"I rode stallions from the mountains to the sea."

"Okay, Ma."

"Nicky, listen to me. I was the only girl with blonde hair in my village. After I was sick, it grew back blonde. I was the only one."

"Come on, Ma."

"How long do I have to stay here?"

The unfamiliar voices became familiar: "Mrs. Elias, most people are very happy here. You must make an effort. It'll be a lot easier for you."

"And for you."

And: "All right, Hasna. I've told your daughter you're not eating. She's going to call your doctor. If you don't eat, she'll put you in the hospital. They stick feeding tubes down your throat. Believe me, Hasna, it's much better here."

✤   ✤   ✤

Then: "Hasna, you can't have valuables here. Things get stolen in spite of all we do. Then we get blamed. I'll put your ring away for you."

"I'll tell my son."

"What are you going to tell him? That you won't follow the rules? You won't eat? Fine then. Don't eat. No lunch for you. Or dinner. Until you give me the ring."

Midweek, Nicholas slipped in for an extra visit. "What's the matter, Ma? Why won't you eat?" Hasna offered him her left hand.

"They took my wedding ring."

Nicky rubbed her finger with his thumb. "Your tattoo," he smiled as he touched the tiny black cross. Her hooded eyes focused on her empty finger, where blotches of red reached to the nail. There were bruises on her wrist.

"They said they're going to keep it so nobody can steal it."

"We'll see about that."

When Nicky replaced the ring on his mother's finger, it slipped on easily, like Cinderella's slipper.

"We're going to fatten you up. You're coming home with me."

✣   ✣   ✣

They had a family meeting at Nicky's house in the suburbs, while Hasna slept on a daybed in one of the girls rooms. They decided she should stay. Nicky's wife said she'd give it a chance; his daughters moved in together.

Hasna did her best. She tried to use the bathroom at night without waking anyone up; she tried to keep track of her medicines. She learned how to watch her programs only if no one else wanted to use the television set. She didn't eat between meals and wished her daughter-in-law would ask her to cook dinner. She found an out-of-the-way chair and crocheted her fingers sore. She did her own laundry (tying up the washing machine for hours). When she helped the girls make yarn dolls, they seemed angry with her for reasons she didn't understand. She started having a cold glass of beer with lunch. With dinner. So she could sleep.

When Nicky came home—and she noticed this didn't occur until very late several nights a week—she wondered if this was why her daughter-in-law rarely smiled at her anymore and she remembered she'd spoiled him as a child. Cooking him his favorite dishes. Always different from what the rest of the family ate. She remembered she'd spanked him with a brush when he cut Elizabeth's hair; she'd spanked them both.

After three months, Nicky said to her one night, "Ma, there's another place we want you to try."

When the truck from the church parked in front of Hasna's house, Louise was waiting for it. Two men in overalls loaded the kitchen table and chairs in the back of the truck and dismembered the old bed with its carved pineapples on the top of each post. They took a break, drinking water from the unmatched mugs that Louise had withdrawn from a taped, cardboard box.

When the truck drove off, the house was empty. Family photographs claimed days before; favorite dishes, mementos, knickknacks. Nicky's wife took the candy dish for her daughters. A few days later a gracious letter arrived at the empty house, thanking Mrs. Joseph Elias, on behalf of St. George's Greek Orthodox Church, for her generous donation of furniture and miscellaneous household items. Louise decided her mother wasn't yet ready for the news.

Joseph collected his mother's mail every day until the trickle dried up. Within a week, an agent pounded a "For

Sale" sign in the front lawn and began taking small, young families through.

Covering the surface of the cupboard door next to Hasna's bed were the greeting cards. Pastel rabbits for Easter and birthday cards (teddy bears from grandchildren, bouquets of flowers from Louise, Joseph, Nicholas; a mannish arrangement of mallard ducks and fishing tackle from Mrs. Caputo, who had died since its sending), Valentine cards, Mother's Day cards. Cards taped over cards.

"I don't want to take off the old ones, honey. I'm afraid the paint'll come off, too."

And Hasna always agreed, although she could barely see the cards now. Her hands told her they were fuzzy or sharp enough for a paper cut, or large or small. Her hands, still agile and capable, miraculously free of the arthritis that inflamed her hips and ankles.

The woman hastily dust-mopped the floor. She sprayed disinfectant in the bathroom, emerging to the sound of water swirling behind her.

"How often do I have to remind you, Hasna? You have to do it every time."

"I forget."

Next, the woman changed the sheets on Hasna's bed

and lowered and polished its railings. She freshened the water in the plastic glass, automatically pointing the straw toward where Hasna sat in her wheelchair.

"In a few minutes, I'll take you down to see your programs. Do you want another drink before we go?"

"Okay."

The woman reached into the back of one of the drawers. "Remember, this is our little secret. You tell anybody and they'll take it away. And I'll lose my job. And there won't be anybody here to give it to you."

Hasna raised the bottle to her mouth and swallowed.

"You're a good girl," said the woman, as she caught the dribbles under Hasna's chin with the back of her hand.

By the time Hasna rolled down the linoleumed hallway, past a shuffling, stooped man, and a line of old women belted upright in their chairs, her head hung groggily to one side.

"Here we are, Hasna."

The woman placed her at the edge of the small assemblage around the television set. Hasna's head bobbed slightly as she adapted, eyes closed, to her new location. The program began and ran its course. There was another program and then another.

Suddenly Hasna woke in the semidarkness. "Nicky," she cried out in confusion. "Nicky."

"Sh-h-h, Hasna, you're disturbing everyone," said the woman, as she pulled the wheelchair to her side and rocked it back and forth until Hasna again fell asleep.

Hasna snored gently. In her dream, she was on a train traveling west, barely noticing the rushing landscape outside her window. In the company of her husband and children—crowded, hungry, expectant. She was disembarking now, into a vast and unknowable place. Her feet in their sturdy shoes addressed the platform. Her slippers, on the footrest of her wheelchair, shifted slightly.